Sally's Sailor

The American West Series

Laura Stapleton

D1468982

ISBN-13: 9781796683899

DEDICATION

To Dallis, Carra, and Keira in our RSTU Mob. We rule!

CONTENTS

ACKNOWLEDGMENTS

I feel very honored to have been asked to write a story for the Alphabet Mail-Order Brides. I've wanted to participate in a project for a long time but the timing never seemed right. Finishing up one book and a family emergency gave me an unexpected chance to join in. This has been a wonderful experience and a huge thanks to all of my author friends.

CHAPTER ONE

Sally Wigg turned a page of *The Bride's Bulletin*. No one appealed to her and she was already halfway through the thin book. "How do we know for sure? No one writing for the *Bulletin* would dare print wife beater, abandoner, or hater. We wouldn't have a clue until after the wedding. I love and trust Madam Wiggie, truly, but..."

"But?" Tillie prompted her.

When Tillie tucked a black lock of hair behind Sally's ear, she glanced up. She didn't want to say aloud how wrong their mentor was in sending them out with strange men. But, Tillie, Uma, and Rebecca all waited for her answer. "I really don't think any of this is a good idea."

Uma groaned. "For goodness sake, Sal, stop dithering and pick one." She rolled her amber-colored eyes and flopped down on a bed. "It's not like we have a choice beyond these men."

Rebecca came up behind Sally to peer over her shoulder. "How about you pray for guidance and then look again?"

Sally sighed. Her taller and fair-haired sister had a standard suggestion for all of life's problems. Good advice, certainly, but God helped those who helped themselves. "I did that the last few times you suggested I do so." She flipped another page. "I'll never find what I want."

Tillie laughed. "What, never?"

She couldn't help but smile at her tease. The four of them had tickets to see *HMS Pinafore* next month. Everyone around them had attended and quoted endlessly from the musical. "No, never!"

"What, *never?*" Uma snickered while writing a letter.

A handsome face stopped her eyes from scanning the rest of the page. She tapped his name with her finger and murmured, "Well, hardly ever." She read the text under his image. Mr. Henry DuBoise, formerly of the Union army and now a sailor on the Columbia River. He sought an independent and strong wife in both mind and body, which she was. He had plans to settle down on a farm, raise a large family, and needed a capable, smart wife. This was her groom. He had to be.

Tillie walked to her. "She found one. It's a miracle."

Uma rolled off the bed to come see, too, and the four girls looked at Henry. "My goodness, he is nice looking. A sailor, too."

Sally glanced from his description back to his photograph, breathless and a little surprised. He seemed perfect except he'd been in the *Union* army? After counting backward, she shook her head. "No. This must be a very old picture of him."

Rebecca took the book. "I see what you mean. He's our age in the photograph. If he had fought in the war, he would have to be at least thirty-one." She peered closer. "Henry here looks like he's twelve."

Uma tsk-tsked. "I don't know. A lot of men lied about their age. One of our cooks fought when he was sixteen, and he's not yet thirty."

Sally retrieved the *Bulletin* from Rebecca who went back to the pile of their mending. She glanced over at Tillie as she settled in next to Rebecca. "Makes sense. He could have been a youngster." When she caught sight of his photo again, her heart did a funny flip-flop. He'd survived battle and had seen some of the United States. Asking him questions about the many states he must have visited would help her future students. Plus, he was terribly handsome.

"He has a good smile," Tillie said while peering at a torn apron. "I wonder if he's ever tried theater."

"Doubtful," Sally replied. "It seems he'd rather be sailing or on a steamboat." She examined the photo a little more closely. He had light hair and light eyes. With black and white newsprint, anything was possible, but she reckoned he was a blue-eyed blonde. Smile lines framed his mouth and she could imagine he'd just heard a joke. With every beat of her heart, she liked him a little more.

"So?"

She glanced up at Uma. "Hm?"

"Are you going to write to him?" She shifted her weight from one foot to the other. "Because there are a few more pages I'd like to see today."

"Oh. Yes, of course." Sally gave her the book.

"Don't worry. If I don't like any of the men on the back of your love's page, I'll rip it out for you," she said while flopping down on her bed. "I probably won't like any of them."

"Now, now." Rebecca glanced up from her sewing. "Positivity in all things."

Uma flipped a page with a, "Hmph."

Sally fluffed up the pillow on her bed before pulling out her letter writing desk from underneath. Setting the sloped wooden box on her lap, she opened the lid to retrieve a sheet of paper, the inkwell, and a pen.

Dear Mr. DuBoise,

I'm sure you've received many letters from interested women per your entry in The Bride's Bulletin. I'd like you to consider my interest as well. I think you'll be a fine husband to a woman who...

Her pen faltered. How could she describe herself? She glanced at the other women. Rebecca was tall but as thin as Sally, Tillie, and Uma were short and slender. Not exactly the strong type when compared to some of the other, more sturdy women at Madam Wiggie's school. She bit her lip and dipped the pen into the inkwell before writing again.

...is strong in all the ways women are, yet tender when necessary.

She nodded, pleased with the wording. If he'd wanted a burly woman to marry, he could have hired help for his boat or ship. She'd have to ask what he sailed on. Maybe he planned on being gone for months at a time, sailing around the world on a clipper or other tall ship. She re-inked her pen. He'd have to reconsider going places without her.

I'd like to know of your sailing experiences during the war. Were you along the Pacific coast or Atlantic? Possibly both? Or maybe you fought on a steamboat on the Mississippi? Where would you like to settle down and farm? How many more years you plan to continue your employ as sailor? I'm sure you have many stories about the places you've sailed. Your life sounds very exciting to me. I look forward to hearing all of them when or if we meet.

She paused. Surely, he would want to know more about her than her penmanship. She mentally catalogued all of her better qualities before resuming the letter.

About me. I enjoy teaching children. My best subjects are Geography and History. My goal is to be a schoolteacher at first and eventually run my own school. I'd like to teach children who need extra help with their education and well-being. Any future husband of mine would need to honor my independence.

I look forward to hearing from you very soon,
Sincerely,
Miss Sally Wigg

Sally sat back with a grin and capped her inkwell. He had said he valued independence. Once he replied, she'd find out how serious he'd been. If Mr. DuBoise wouldn't allow her the freedoms he'd indicated in his description, she'd need to rethink her decision. She shuddered at the thought of going back to the *Bulletin* and starting all over.

The three girls had left the room without her noticing. The *Bulletin* lay where Uma left it, so she retrieved the booklet and found where to send her letter. A few minutes later, the ink on the addressed enveloped dried. She put away her portable desk and went to the bedroom door. Her knees trembled a little when she stepped into the hallway.

So many more questions came to mind, in addition to the ones she'd written him. What if he were the worst sort of man? What if he'd used a better-looking friend's image? What if he were truly an elderly man instead of one in his early thirties? In that case, how would she afford to turn around and go home?

Sally shook her head. Nothing mattered right now besides finding a good man to marry. Madam Wiggie depended on her. Some of the other girls in their home had found success. She simply had to believe she would, too.

CHAPTER TWO

Henry DuBoise paced on the train depot's platform. Sally's letter burned a hole in his pocket. Would he know her when he saw her? Would he have to guess which lady was her? He clenched and unclenched his fists to dispel his nervousness.

She'd written such intelligent letters to him in the past few weeks. Each one seemed as if she couldn't tell him enough about her life nor could she read enough about him. She learned he'd been at the tail end of the Civil War. He'd learned she grew up in a New York City school with her sisters. She'd worked to become a schoolteacher, as hard as he had, while manning the fishing boats on the Columbia River. He looked forward to how well they'd make a good team and a great couple.

He lifted the brim of his hat and scratched his damp forehead. The warm fall sun heated the black felt. Nervousness over meeting Sally didn't help. He studied each woman departing the passenger car. One was too old and the girls with her were too young. Others carried babies or led little children as they disembarked. A trio of much older ladies chatted and laughed. They seemed disinterested in a lone man waiting on the platform.

A young lady stepped off of the train with a carpetbag in one gloved hand and her peach colored skirt gathered in the other. Her bonnet matched her dress. Pretty, but far too impractical for country life. He couldn't help but smile at his younger sister, Francine's, influence. She'd be proud of him for noticing.

Or, maybe not so much, since Henry went on to notice her slim but curvy form, as well. The lady was refined and stunning. He watched as she chatted with an engineer, her hair twisting in one long dark curl down her back. He'd need to tell Francine about the newest hair style before she saw anyone else wearing it. Shifting from one foot to the other, he needed to stop staring at the beautiful woman and continue his search for Miss Wigg.

Except, she turned to face him and took a few steps forward. As she approached, he noticed she had the clearest gray-blue eyes he'd ever seen, a rosebud mouth, and the fairest skin. He smiled. She'd need that bonnet or there'd be freckles gracing her pretty nose in a week. Her intent expression gave way to a large grin he couldn't help but return.

"Mr. DuBoise!" She dropped her skirt to hold out a hand. "You look exactly like your photograph."

After taking her hand, he realized she had to be his Sally. "Miss Wigg?" he croaked. Holding her slender fingers in his calloused ones, his heart sunk to his feet. There was no way in God's green Earth this woman could ever be a farm wife. No way at all.

"I am." She shook his hand, the smile never

leaving her face. "It is such a pleasure. I must confess, I had apprehensions about your age and temperament." She let go of him, her cheeks turning pink. "Your photograph doesn't do you justice. You are far more handsome in person."

"I, well, I agree," he stammered. Oh Lord. The woman considered him attractive, too. "That's not what I meant. Er, if you had a photograph of you, you'd be prettier than it would say you were." He coughed. "Or something. I don't know." Her face reddened even more. She stared down at her feet, the brim of her hat blocking her upper face from his view.

"I'm glad you think so, since I had concerns. One never knows about a friendship until meeting face to face."

Her sudden shyness endeared her to him. "You're quite lovely, miss, and it's a pleasure to meet you." He sighed in relief as soon as the words were out. They were all in the right order and made sense.

Sally glanced up with a smile. "Thank you." She moved her carpetbag from one hand to the other. "Should we eat lunch before or after we're married?"

Married? Henry stopped breathing for a moment. Her question meant they were supposed to be man and wife by bedtime tonight. He had plans for getting to know each other for a little while. Then, they'd continue his search for a farm to own. He held her delicate hand with his rough one. Miss Sally Wigg might be an excellent school teacher, but she'd never make a good farmer's wife. "Um, about that. We need to talk."

"Oh. Sounds very ominous." She glanced around at the empty train platform. "Should we talk here and now, or later?"

Henry thought for a second or two. He'd seen war. Watched grown men scream as they lay dying. Rushed to take down an enemy ship before being taken down themselves. Yet, the thought of making Sally cry, out here in public, made his stomach curdle. "Let's have lunch and discuss our future, shall we?"

"I'd like that." She took his arm. "I'll need you to show me the way until I become acquainted with my new hometown." Falling in step with him, she continued, "Everything is so much different than New York City. The buildings are all wood. Not a stone in sight."

He led her onto the boardwalk and half listened to her describing cobblestone streets. She went on about the smoke and fog, the crowds, and all the various unclean smells. Meanwhile, all he could think about was how to tell her she couldn't stay here and marry him.

Henry gave her another side-glance while they walked past Granville & Sons law offices. The woman was simply too beautiful, delicate, and overall perfect to ever labor on the beginnings of a farm. He stared ahead. Scratch that. She was too perfect to be *his* wife. The woman deserved a far easier life than he could or would provide. Especially if he ended up being like Pa.

"Is this the hotel?"

Her voice startled him out of his daydream. "Hm?" He looked up at the sign for The Oregonian Hotel. "Right. We're here." He opened the door for her. "Sorry. I was enthralled by your story."

Sally stepped inside and gave a backward glance at him with a smile. "I don't think I've ever enthralled someone before. Thank you for the compliment."

"My pleasure." He removed his hat and ran a hand through his hair. "We can sit anywhere."

"How about at a window? I'd like to see the people who live here." She led the way to large ceiling to knee height windows. "It's probably all the same to you, though. You're used to everything being so new."

In his shock over Sally's appearance, he'd forgotten to indulge her in some sightseeing. "I know exactly where we should sit." Hat in hand, he showed her his favorite table.

The dining room wasn't crowded. Most of the people there for lunch had been and gone. He stared at everything as if the restaurant was new to him. Sunlight gleamed off of place settings and vases held fresh flowers. Yep, he'd chosen the place wisely. No one would kick up a fuss about being sent back home in such a fine establishment. Plus, he liked The Oregonian's food.

While a young waiter hovered nearby, Henry pulled the chair out for her. He took the opportunity to find his own seat and say, "Two waters, please."

The boy nodded and gave them each a menu. Sally waited until he was out of earshot before leaning in toward Henry. "I don't think I've ever been to a place so fancy."

He smiled, or tried to. "Lunch here isn't a habit for me. I'd rather have a simpler meal and save money for the future."

Sally frowned and put down the menu. "Should we go elsewhere? I don't mind helping you reach our goals."

Henry winced. *Our* goals? He was focused on the

farm, but her…she needed to focus on someone else.

"What's wrong?" she asked just as the waiter returned with their drinks.

"Thank you," Henry said. "I'll have the chicken fried steak and so will the lady." He glanced at Sally, a little surprised to see her frown before giving the menu to their waiter. With a start, he realized he'd been rude in presuming what she wanted, but the steak was exceptional, with the best gravy.

"Very good, sir."

After watching him leave, he smiled at Sally. "I'm sorry. I should have asked you first, but the meal is their best."

"I'm sure it is. Thank you for ordering for me."

"You're welcome." Waiting for her to add anything more, he followed her gaze out of the window. People and wagons went by, all in a rush to get somewhere. Every year, the population grew and, every year, he wanted to escape living in town.

Henry gave her a side glance. The speech he needed to plan about her going anywhere else and forgetting he existed could be given after the meal. He didn't want them sitting in stony silence and choking down food. "My sister's family lives outside of town, closer to Oregon City than here. I'd like my farm to be near them."

Sally refocused on him. "Do you know of anyone ready to sell to you?"

"Not yet." He smiled at her. "Several people live near Ellen and Del's home. Any one of them would be good for what I want." He paused before going further. All Miss Wigg needed to know was her way back home, because he wasn't marrying her.

They both waited until the server placed their

meals and asked, "Do you need anything else?"

Henry glanced at Sally's full water glass before answering, "No, thank you." As soon as the young man left the area, they began eating. Neither one of them said anything else until he glanced down and saw half of his steak was gone. "I must be hungrier than I thought."

She swallowed before tearing apart her dinner roll. "I agree. Breakfast seems to have been days ago." Slathering butter on her bread, she asked, "Weren't we going to have a serious talk?"

Henry put down his silverware. "I suppose now is as good a time as any." He wiped his mouth with the napkin and stared at her. The first words in his mind popped out. "You are the most beautiful woman I've ever seen." She opened her mouth to say something and he held up a hand. "But, I can't marry you and here's why."

Despite his inner qualms over her reddening face and narrowed eyes, Henry continued. "If you'll remember, I advertised for someone strong and sturdy. No offence, ma'am, but you're neither."

"I see."

"No, I don't think you do." Before he could change his mind, he said, "I need a wife who can plow, feed chickens, and slop hogs. She'll need to cook a pie in the morning and give birth to my children in the afternoon." Her eyebrows rose at his last few words and his face grew hot at what he'd said aloud. "Or at night. Whenever babies are born. The point is, you'll make a good schoolteacher, sweet and delicate as you are. Just not a good farmer's wife. Not for me."

Sally stared at him for a couple of seconds before

tears filled her eyes. "I didn't lie to you," she said while putting down her knife and fork. The silverware clattered against her plate. "I can do anything a farmer's wife can." She looked up at him. "I could probably do anything a farmer himself can, given the right tools for the job."

Henry's jaw dropped before he began chuckling at the idea of her butchering a hog in that dress. The lady was optimistic, he'd give her that. "I don't think so, darlin'. You may be full of lessons and back east ideas, but you couldn't be a farmer." He stretched a little before waving off the waiter's questioning look. "No, I think it'd be best if we parted as friends and you found a city boy to marry."

"Very well." She pushed the plate away from her. "I don't like admitting this, but while I can pay for my meal, I don't have enough for a train ticket home."

"No one's saying you have to go all the way back to New York City. Go anywhere you like." He paused, not certain he wanted to say the next few words. As if controlled by an outside force, he added, "Or, stay here in Portland and find some dandy man to marry. There's plenty of bankers and businessmen."

"Excellent idea." She began searching her carpetbag. "Since I don't have funds for a reputable hotel, I'll need a place to stay."

He held up his hands as if to slow her down in asking him for anything. "Not with me. My apartment is too small and has only one bed."

She paused in counting her coins. "Hmm." Her lips pursed together for a few seconds before she said, "I understand. Despite what you believe, I happen to be a strong and versatile person. I have no qualms about sleeping in the train depot or resting in a hotel lobby until a teaching position presents itself."

Sally placed six quarters on the table and gave him a steely glare. "You are not the only one with a dream, Mr. DuBoise. I have one as well, and will do whatever I have to in order to make it happen."

He shook his head at her far-fetched idea. "You can't sleep in train stations and hotel lobbies."

"Oh?" She stood and pushed in her chair. "Are you saying so because you're my husband or are you merely a random stranger imposing his will on me?"

Henry wanted to argue they were more acquaintances than strangers, yet, the woman was right. Apart from a few letters and an instant attraction, they didn't know each other at all.

"Since we're at an impasse, I'll bid you good day."

CHAPTER THREE

Sally walked out of the restaurant with her chin up. She was absolutely not going to look back to see if Henry was following her. No sir. She opened her own door and stepped out onto the boardwalk.

Nothing about him mattered any more. Not his ready smile, his politeness to everyone around him, and especially not his dreams of a farm. His clean white shirt fooled no one, nor did his pressed pants. He might look nice but he wasn't—by a long shot.

She walked, each foot heavy on the boards. Where she ended up today didn't matter so long as she put a lot of space between her and Henry. He didn't trust her to be a good wife no matter where they lived. A gust of wind between buildings threatened to lift her hat from her head. She clamped a hand down on her crown and continued.

When he'd mentioned their children, she could have melted right there. After a sigh, Sally paused before someone jostled her into moving again. The content in his letters never wavered with what kind of woman he wanted. She was able to admit liking the idea of a farm with chicks, calves, and foals. She shook herself out of the beginnings of a daydream and glanced around her. The train depot had been in the other direction. "Oh, buttersticks," she said and turned around into a solid wall of man. "Excuse me, I am so sorry." She looked up to see Henry. "Um. Again. Excuse me." She walked around him.

He grabbed her arm. "Hold on, ma'am."

She gave him Madam Wigg's best shaming stare while looking at his face first, then where he held her. He dropped his grip with a flush staining his cheeks. "I mean, I'll walk you to wherever you'd like to go."

"How charitable." She let the sarcasm flow. "I'm so glad you could take time out of your non-married day to help me do something I'm perfectly capable of doing myself." She took several steps forward, saying as he caught up, "You can accompany me to the station. I'll wait there and come up with a new plan."

"All right.

They walked for a while. His diligence in blocking her from accidental knocks didn't escape her attention. If not for his foolish resolve to marry some burly woman, they'd be enjoying an afternoon of wedded bliss together.

She smiled a little at what Henry might say if she reminded him of what being married meant. Madam Wiggie hadn't left them completely ignorant of what happened after the vows. She glanced at him and his determined face. None of the former students at Madam Wiggie's, who'd left and written back, had mentioned negotiating for more engagement time with their prospective grooms.

They approached the station and she stopped him. "Thank you for seeing me here. You may go. I'll be fine."

He shrugged. "I might go along and wait with you for a while. My next work shift is tomorrow afternoon."

Sally hid a smile over the new crack in his little stone of a heart. Surely, he wasn't going to change his mind, was he? She gave him a shrug and led the way into the quiet depot. "It's your time to waste." No one sat in the pew-like benches. Their footsteps echoed on the tile floor. "At least it's clean and still smells like new lumber."

"I can't tell how new the building is." He sat down and patted the bench beside him. "The depot is old for this part of the country."

"Hmm." She looked around at the ornate moldings bordering the doors and windows. Maybe Henry couldn't smell the sap anymore, but she could. She tilted her head. Architecture was interesting but appreciating it now wouldn't get her a teaching position. She dug around in her carpetbag for a pencil and her journal. Henry shifted beside her.

"Do you need help with planning?"

A very unladylike snort came out before Sally thought to stop it. "No. I think you've altered my plans far more than any railroad bandit or bridge washout could have done." She opened her journal to a back page, unwilling to crowd her lesson plans written in the front. "I just want to make a list of priorities for today."

"Smart," he said and when she looked at him, he smiled. "Understandable since you're a school marm and all." He started staring at her blank page. "You'll need a place to stay."

"Um hm." She wrote down the number one and

"living quarters" after it. "Which is good, but I'll need employment." She scribbled down the words work, food, and transportation with a question mark after it.

"Yep. You'll need all of those."

A little annoyed with his over the shoulder reading, she stopped and stared at him; maybe providence had been wise in delaying their marriage. Though irritating, she supposed he was trying to be helpful in a dim way. "Where do you live?"

"We're not getting married."

She closed her eyes. His unending refusals were beginning to sting her feelings. "I understand. However, if you live in an inexpensive place because you're saving for a farm and if your landlord has additional places to rent, I'm interested."

"Oh." He reclined against the back of the bench. "Good point. My place is small. One bedroom. You're right in that it's cheap but they don't rent to single women. Too much trouble."

Avoiding the urge to argue about which gender was a problem in the world, she asked, "Do they rent to married people?"

"Sure. We would have lived there if today worked out for us."

She nodded and stared at the page. They could live there together after a marriage ceremony. The day was still young. Except, if she asked Henry for even a sham of a marriage, he'd probably go into fits about his dreams again.

Sally reexamined the depot. The place wasn't bad. Clean, quiet most of the time. Others in her orphanage had slept in far worse conditions. She'd arrived as an infant while other children were brought in off of the city streets. They would have loved a bed as nice as her seat. She ran her fingertips down the smooth wood. Her bag made a nice pillow until someone protested her sleeping there.

"I have an idea," Henry said. "Think about it before you refuse."

"Go on."

He rubbed a hand down his face as if to scrub away the stress. "How about we get married like we'd planned, but in name only. That way, you have a place to live and I can have my farm wife later when you're settled somewhere else."

Sally frowned. "Would you want an eventual divorce? I don't think I can teach while married or as a divorcee, until I begin my own school, that is." She sat up straighter and tapped her pencil tip against the journal. "Although, we could have an annulment. It'll be as if the marriage never happened."

"An annulment sounds good. You have a place to stay and could do wifely duties until..." he trailed off. "I mean, you could keep the apartment clean, maybe wash clothes, and cook dinner once in a while? That's all I meant."

Sally grinned at his backtracking. "I can take care of your home while I'm there. I'm sure it won't be a long stay. All I need is an interview with a superintendent. Madam Wiggie, um, Wigg, wrote me an excellent recommendation letter."

"Then it's settled." Henry stood and held out a hand to her. "We'll go to the courthouse, get married, and you'll have somewhere to sleep tonight besides here."

She took his support to stand up with him. His smile pulled an answering grin from her. "Thank you. I do appreciate your help. Don't worry about being turned out of your bed. I can sleep anywhere."

"No lady like you will sleep on my floor." He linked his arm with hers to lead her out of the depot. "Besides, I don't mind sharing a bed with you."

Sally gave him a quick glance. They'd never even kissed and he'd mentioned sleeping together twice today? He was either a cheeky devil or didn't really see her as a woman. She cleared her throat in the dusty air. "The floor is fine. I can make a pallet of blankets."

He held the door open for her. "Nonsense. We can take those blankets and roll them up as a divider. My bed's plenty big enough for your side and my side."

"Good." She didn't know how to feel about his lack of interest. His quick problem solving skills to keep them apart stung a little, too. No one wanted a spouse who didn't find her appealing.

She snuck another glance at him while they waited to cross the street. When they first met, his eyes had lit up. Interest showed in his face before he knew who she was. If she could prove to him her capabilities, he'd want to keep her as more than a mock wife.

Henry led her to the other side of the street and nodded to their right. "I checked around for the justice of the peace. His office is straight ahead."

"So you really had planned on marrying me today." Hope filled her again. Once they were married, he'd have a tougher time forcing his indifference to her. She smiled up at him. "I don't mind a later annulment as long as you don't, either."

"Not as long as you'll let me keep my advertisement in *The Bride's Bulletin*. I'll need to write it, of course. Make it clear I need a farmhand of a wife instead of a fashion plate."

Sally's smile faded as she swallowed a hard lump of anger. "Your advert was accurate and I am no fashion plate of a woman. I am a hard worker, a quick student, and an excellent teacher. Your lack of appreciation for my...*everything*, is solely your fault. Not mine." She lifted her chin and looked down her nose at him. "Now, if you don't mind, let's get this farce of a marriage started so we can end it just as quickly."

She stepped forward and opened the door without waiting for him. Gripping her bag so hard her fingers ached, she approached the only person in the room. "Hello. I'd like to obtain a marriage license today."

An older man behind a counter glanced up with a smile. "Sure thing, miss." He looked past her for a moment. "I suppose you want to marry this river rat?"

Not favoring Henry with a backward glance, she nodded. "Yes, please."

He chuckled and opened a large book to his right. "I figured as much. He'd been loitering around here all morning, eager to get hitched, and now I see why."

"How sweet." A sarcasm she couldn't help laced her words. She turned to Henry as he removed his hat. "You're such a romantic."

"Only the best for you, dearest." Henry leaned against the counter. "How is Mrs. Martin?"

The clerk laid a document in front of Sally. "Here's the form. Fill it out but don't sign. That'll be later and in front of witnesses." He mirrored Henry's lean. "The missus is fine. Fretting about Ben finding a good woman to settle down with."

She nodded while the two talked about people she didn't know. If he'd even hinted at them staying married beyond next month, she'd pay attention and learn more about his friends. Instead, she ignored their gossip.

Sally read over the paper. The words were so official and seemed far too real. An inkwell and waiting pen lay to the side so she scooted the document and herself over to begin writing her name.

"The fee is two dollars," the clerk added in the middle of his monologue.

Sally glanced up. "So much?" She'd have to take off her bonnet to retrieve the money from a hidden pocket.

He shrugged. "It's a test of your commitment."

Henry pulled a couple of dollars from his pocket. "Well worth the price, isn't it, sweetheart?"

She uncorked the inkwell and struggled for diplomacy. "Of course it is, darling. You hadn't mentioned the fee earlier or I would have paid my share."

"Nonsense. You spent enough on the trip." He took the pen from her. "The least I can do is pay for our wedding."

Sally took a step back to give him room. She watched as he filled in his information; his full name as Henry Jackson DuBoise. A more romantic day might have left her daydreaming about their children's names. Now all she wanted to do was sign the document and learn where she now lived.

Before the ink dried, the clerk hollered, "Ben! Get in here and witness." After a scuffle, a young, thin man came out of a back room.

Having seen his expression on several of the

orphanage students, she tried not to smile. He'd either been sleeping or studying.

"Yeah, Pa." He ambled over to the counter. "I'm ready."

Henry waited for a nod from the clerk before signing his name on the bottom line with a flourish. He handed the pen to her. His hand didn't shake as much as hers did as she re-dipped the pen into the inkwell. She steadied her nerves by remembering how the document meant nothing. They'd be strangers in a few weeks, God willing. She signed Sarah Louise Wigg on her line.

"Sarah?" Henry asked. "I didn't know your name was Sarah. It's pretty."

"Sally, please," she told him in her best schoolteacher voice. She turned to the clerk and Ben. "Is that all? How long do we need to wait for the marriage to take effect?"

He looked from her to Henry. "Well, I usually say a few words about marriage and what it means. Then there's blessing the union."

She looked from one man to the other. "What does that mean?"

Ben snickered and the clerk gave him a glare. "It's pretty simple. I say bless this union and these two people."

"Ah, very good," she said and tried not to smile at the impatient expression on Henry's face.

"And the kiss is last. Sort of like a good luck charm for the marriage. Until death do you part is a lot easier if there's a solid kiss in the beginning." He shrugged. "To be honest, I usually just file the paperwork after the church wedding. Every once in a while there's a small ceremony here." He turned to his son. "When was our last wedding?"

Ben didn't glance up while folding up the license before placing it in an envelope. "I don't know. Ma probably witnessed it, not me," he added while writing down the information in the book to the clerk's side.

"Around three years ago, then."

Henry nudged her and grinned. "Not a lot of women are as lucky as you are, with a man eager to marry them like this. I haven't had your cooking or even a kiss today."

She ignored Ben and Henry's chuckling. When was the last time she'd noticed anyone kissing? Mashing lips together seemed rather easy if not somewhat disgusting. But, if it meant she had a place to stay until getting a teaching assignment, she needed to play the part. Plus… She gave a side-glance to her new husband. She'd wanted to try kissing him from the first moment they'd met. After biting her lip, her face grew warmer as she said, "If we're paying the full price of two dollars, we might as well get the whole package."

The clerk stood straighter. "There you go, Henry. The little woman is already getting you your dollars' worth." He placed his hands on the counter. "Marriage is a blessed union. One does not step into the bonds of holy matrimony lightly or with frivolity. One must think of the other, in sickness and health, for a long as you both are, well, both are one."

Ben snickered and the clerk gave him a glare before continuing. "I bless this union and pray these two fine young people live their lives together in happiness." He nodded at Henry. "You may kiss the bride."

Sally looked up at Henry. His clean-shaven face and dry lips helped ease her apprehension. He smelled good when leaning in toward her, so she tilted her chin up a little more to meet him halfway. When they met, her entire body tingled as if full of static electricity. She moaned in response and he wrapped his arms around her. Their bodies pressed together, she parted her lips a little. Her pulse hammered in her ears. His body hard against hers, every sinewy muscle pressed against her softness.

One of their witnesses let out a low whistle, breaking the spell. Henry pulled away from her. "I reckon we're married enough now." He set her away from him and smiled at the clerk. "Thank you, Mr. Martin. Say hello to Mrs. Martin and Gwen for me."

"Will do, and congratulations. You two make a fine couple."

"Appreciate it." Henry turned to her and his smile faded. "Let's go home, wife."

She tried to be genuine with her smile. "Certainly, husband." He led the way out and she followed.

Once the door closed, he turned to her. "I'm going anywhere else in the county to file our annulment."

In a flash, she empathized with him. She could slip away since everyone, including her new husband, was a stranger. She reached out for his arm. "It's difficult when you know them personally."

"You said it." He ignored her hand and mashed down his hat. "Let's go home. You might as well know where you're living for the next day or so."

Her heart skipped a beat. She had faith in her abilities but what if the search took a week or more? He was walking on so she hurried to fall in step with him. She rushed to keep up with him, since his stride was far longer than hers." A little out of breath, she asked, "How far is it to your place?"

He gave her a brief look but didn't slow down any. "Not far. A mile or so."

Her last chance to freshen up had been hours ago and crossing her fingers, she asked, "Do you have a kitchen or water closet?"

"Water closet?" He stopped for a second before continuing. "No. Just a stove, a couple of dressers, and shelves. I'd like to get an icebox for the new house someday."

She nodded even though he wasn't looking at her. Dust seemed to coat the inside of her mouth, so she tried to breathe through her nose. "I would, too."

He kept walking on as if not caring that she'd replied. Sally hurried to keep up. Panic bubbled up in her stomach every time some intervening person blocked her view of him. Out of breath, she stopped and leaned against a lamppost. She had no idea what she'd do if he left her behind. Maybe wait by his post office box or search the docks for him. Or, she could just let him go and live her life. Truly be married in name only. The stitch in her side continued as she tried to keep from gasping for air. She almost didn't care when his hat disappeared among the throng of people.

Once her heart calmed down to a normal beat, she stood upright. He had continued on so she would, too. Another group of apartments or a hostel must be near his. She frowned. Not that she wanted to ever see him again, but a place to stay tonight would be nice.

Sally began walking at her own pace yet still didn't dawdle. What worried her the most was if Henry turned down a side street, she'd never see him again. She faltered a little in her stride before regaining her march forward. Any man who'd leave her behind after a kiss like they'd had wasn't worth spit. She was better off returning to live on the streets of New York City.

CHAPTER FOUR

"There you are!"

Sally turned to see Henry leaning against a doorway entrance. She frowned at his relieved tone. He slouched against the wooden post, too attractive for her to hate him, much. "Yes? So?"

He stood up straighter and took a step toward her. "I was waiting for you."

"Oh?" She kept her voice frosty. The last thing she'd do is fawn over his doing the bare minimum. "Anything could have happened in the few minutes you'd left me behind."

"Sorry. I got lost trying to think up a way to explain myself, ourselves." He stepped down to her. "The whole mess of today."

She crossed her arms. "I agree. It's been horrible so far."

"Yeah, well, let's just look to the future where we each get what we want and life is back to normal." He put a hand on her shoulder and squeezed. "Agreed?"

His touch melted her irritation as if she were made of soft snow. She nodded. "Agreed."

"This is my building, by the way." He went back up the steps and opened the door for her. "Not the entire thing, of course. My room is the only part I own and even that is month to month."

"Room?" She bit her lip and followed him up the narrow stairs. If his home was small, she'd have nowhere to go after an argument without bumping into him.

"A single. The least expensive here." Henry unlocked the door for her. "I cleaned it up especially for today."

Sally stepped into the apartment and she let out her pent up breath. The room seemed spacious compared to what she, Tillie, Uma, and Rebecca had shared. A wood stove stood to the right with a table-high dresser next to it. She walked in further. The bed, dining table, and a larger chest of drawers took up what remained of the area. Thin curtains covered the nearly floor to ceiling windows facing west. "The sunsets must be magnificent."

"They are." The door clicked shut and the lock turned before he continued, "Or, they are until a new, taller building goes up."

"That would be a shame." She turned to him. "Have you ever had a roommate?"

"No, and I'd thought about asking around." He hung his hat over a coat on the peg rack near the door. "After all day around people on a barge, I'm ready to be alone for a while." He slipped off his jacket and laid it on the bed while leaving his vest on over his shirt.

She nodded, understanding the sentiment. "Sometimes, I'd find a closet to rest in for a few minutes before facing all of the other girls in the school."

He went over and opened the top drawer in a dresser. "I have a place cleaned out for you here. It's not much, but I'd planned on more in the new home." He stood aside and watched as she unpacked her belongings. "There's not much I remember about Missouri, and most of the east I saw was from a war ship. Is New York City as crowded as it seems?"

"So far, Oregon isn't as populous as my home. Our ideas probably differ over what's new and what's old. I suspect you would think a thin crowd is too much." She put her nightgown on top of her work dress. "Everyone seems happier here yet still as busy." Her journal and pencil lay to the side of her clothes. She gave him a glance. He still leaned against the wall, watching. Unpacking her underclothes could wait until he left the apartment.

He leaned over and peered in at her belongings. "Is that all? I figured as fancy as the dress you're wearing is, you'd have a couple more."

"No, I have my Sunday dress and my work dress." She smiled and set her carpetbag to the side with her bonnet on top. "I'm sure one day this will become my everyday clothes."

"Hmm, I reckon so." He walked over to the thinner dresser. "If you're hungry, I have dry goods in here. Water and the outhouse are down the stairs and at the back of the building." He shrugged. "I just go outside instead of keeping a chamber pot in the house."

Her face heated at the mention. "I understand. Carrying out the night soil is the worst chore at our school."

He laughed and put on a dustier, older coat from

under his hat. "The worst anywhere. Make yourself at home. The pitcher has fresh water from this morning."

She frowned when seeing him reach for the door. "Are you leaving?"

"I am." He paused at the doorway for a moment. "I guess part of having a wife is letting her know where I'll be." He smiled and walked over to her. "A few of the crew is meeting up down at Shorty's for a game of cards. It's the captain's birthday and he's buying."

"Oh." Sally wasn't sure if she should be worried or not. "Is this a once a week or once a year event?"

"More like once a quarter since we all have birthdays to celebrate. They'll find any excuse for Shorty's." He began to lean toward her but stopped and tapped his hat against his thigh. "I won't be gone long. Everything in here is yours, too, so don't be shy if you need something."

"I won't." She followed him to the door. "Did you want me to save some dinner for you?"

"Naw. There's always something to eat over there. Peanuts, fried potatoes, popcorn." He unlocked and opened the door. "Shorty's always keeping us thirsty."

Sally smiled. "Smart businessman."

"Yep." He looked down the hall. "So, I'll be home later."

"All right," she said. The door's lock clicked and she smiled. He wasn't the typical groom, no, but he did consider her security. Or, he had a good habit. Either way, she liked the peace and quiet to sort out the upheaval of today.

Sally went to her hat next to the clothes dresser and checked the inner lining out of habit. All of her money was still there, of course. She hadn't expected the bills to evaporate, but still. One never knew. Accidents happened every day.

She wedged the hat between her bag and the furniture holding the rest of her belongings. The brim might need straightening later but too bad. She didn't want Henry to suspect she had the money to return home. Between her hard work and Madam Wigg's generosity, the funds would create her school. Then, she could focus on her new marriage with Henry. He needed to see how he was much better off with her as his wife.

The bed took up most of the small room and she had avoided looking in its direction while Henry was here. She walked over and sat on the overly large piece of furniture. The mattress was soft under her and tempted her into lying down for a rest. She stood and shook off the drowsiness.

Like anyone, Henry would probably love to come home to dinner already prepared for him. Shorty had snacks, not a decent meal. And anyway, he might not be hungry tonight, but she was. The sun sank low behind another building and gave a chill to the room. She made a quick search of his makeshift pantry. After putting a couple of handfuls of rice and beans into a pot, she added a few pinches of salt and peppercorns. She checked the stove and began the fire.

Henry hadn't left her a key, so she didn't want to leave the apartment. She went over to the washbasin and pitcher. If a person washed their hands and face from here, she figured the water was clean enough for cooking, too. She poured in enough water to cook the food.

Satisfied dinner was cooking, Sally went to the stack of books beside the bed. Henry had them piled on top of each other in a makeshift night table. She picked the topmost one titled *Spruner Atlas Antiquus*. The page fell open to a map of the world. A bookmark lay in the middle with various countries written on it. She smiled and wondered if Henry ever planned on traveling so far and wide, or if these were places he'd already been. Wanting to know more, she started at the beginning of the book and paged through the various maps.

The shadows lengthened until the room dimmed in last traces of twilight. She looked up in the semi darkness and her stomach growled. The beans and rice smelled good. She hopped up and hurried to the warm stove. They hadn't burned because she hadn't stoked the logs. She sighed and rebuilt the fire. Dinner might be done by the morning, if then.

She stirred the pot while giving the rest of the books a hard stare. *The Underground Railroad* and *The Steam Powered Man* would have to wait. Once satisfied with the simmering food, she retrieved her journal and a pencil. Henry had matches and a lantern on the table, and soon she had plenty of light to write a brief summary of the day.

Sally turned to the back of the book and reviewed her list of things to do. She had a place to sleep tonight. Food cooked on the stove. Tomorrow, she'd search for a teaching position to help raise funds for her school and Henry's farm. She closed her journal and put her head in her hands for a few minutes.

Her stomach growled again. Taking her body's hint, she put away her things and ate. She put his dinner in a bowl and poured the rest of the wash water into the pan. Gas streetlights pushed away the pitch black outside. She wished Henry had gone to the trouble of a chamber pot after all. Hoping no one walked into the apartment during her absence, she hurried to the outhouse in back, doing her business, and refilling the water.

Once back in the apartment, she locked the door. She changed into bedclothes without delay and washed her face and hands. Henry hadn't rolled up a blanket to put between them, so she did the task for them both. She'd take the side against the wall so he'd not have to climb over her to sleep.

She turned down the lamp and crawled in under the covers. He'd be back soon, surely, and she could ask about washing clothes, dishes, moping, and other cleaning he'd want done. She yawned and cuddled deeper into the soft bed.

A loud crash woke her. She froze, hoping Henry had come home. After a slight thud followed by a recognizable masculine chuckle, she relaxed. She had no idea of the time but the hour had to be late. "Henry? Are you hurt?"

"Aw, nuts. I woke you. Sorry, darlin'."

She could see him in the moonlight streaming in from outside. He sat on his side of the bed. First one boot, thudded to the floor, then the other. "Did you have a good time?" she asked before the smell hit her. Whiskey, and a lot of it.

"I did, thank you." He lay down, still fully dressed. "Something in here smells good. What did you cook?"

"Um," she began before the heavy liquor odor took her breath. "Rice and beans. There's some left over on the stove."

He sighed and put an arm over his eyes. "You're such a good wife. So pretty, sweet, kind, and a little feisty. I told the boys all about you tonight. About how you'd be perfect with twenty-five to fifty pounds more weight and a few inches of height."

Her entire body froze and chill bumps broke out over her skin. He had gotten drunk before blabbing about their sham marriage to his wharf friends? She sunk in lower under the covers. She'd asked about his opinion on liquor and remembered his answer. Clearing her throat, she said, "You never hinted in your letters about being a drunk, Mr. DuBoise."

CHAPTER FIVE

Henry's cloud of happiness dissipated like a fog during a desert afternoon. "What? I'm not at all a drunk."

"You smell like one."

Sally had him there. Two shots of whiskey and spilled ale had left him reeking. He could tell her what occurred but she didn't seem to be in a listening mood. "Accidents happen." He rolled over to face away from her. "We can talk about tonight in the morning."

She turned away from him with a hard tug at the covers and the bedroll jostled between them. "We don't need to talk about anything at all."

He smiled at her irritation. Earlier, when he'd told the boys about a spirited girl he'd met, the admission surprised him. Any man with eyes would find Sally beautiful, but he appreciated her drive to better her situation. He yawned and folded the covers over his body. She'd hear all about tonight and the frivolity tomorrow when she was in a better mood.

Early the next morning, each slam of the oven

door reverberated in his skull. "Stop," he muttered. "Go away."

"Good morning," she all but sang to him.

He tried to open an eye. Sunlight blasted in through shadeless windows. The air smelled good but the warmth pressed down like a huge fist on his chest. At first, a hot sweat broke out over his body, followed by shivering chills. He sat up and the room spun. "I think I caught a fever of some sort."

"Oh?" She smacked a frying pan down on the stove. "You don't think it's whiskey-itis?" She poured a couple of cups of coffee, letting the pot smack against the burner. "Because your clothes, breath, and everything else tells me that's why you're feeling poorly."

He took the cup she offered and closed his eyes. "Probably. Shaky bought rounds for us and I stopped at two." All he wanted was for the hammering in his head to stop already. Her clanking around didn't help. Maybe a steamboat whistle would be quieter than her opening and closing his pantry drawers. Something began sizzling and he smelled ham.

"Two what? Gallons."

He laughed at her sarcasm, stopping short at the resulting ache. "You'd be a lot funnier if I were in less pain."

"Everything would be better if you hadn't gone out last night."

Her sharp tone made him stare up at her. No way was a woman ordering him around like a lap dog. "You're not keeping me from my friends."

"No, you're right. I'm not." She flipped over the meat. "You're a free man. I would just ask you to be sober when I need you to be."

The words hit him in soft spots no one in the world knew he had. "I'm always sober. Usually."

"Um hm."

Her little disbelieving tone irritated Henry but he couldn't blame her. He'd spent their wedding night at the tavern without her. "I'm sorry." He took a sip and looked into the cup. Even queasy, he liked her coffee better than his own. "I'll bring you along next time."

Sally laughed. "As if I'd go." She shook her head and plated up her breakfast. "No. Waking up like you is not my idea of fun."

"I had a good time until this morning." He rubbed his temple in an effort to ease the throbbing. "We played cards for beans. I won."

"Good for you. Next time play for money and we'll both be happy."

"Really? You'd want me to gamble with money?" Using some of his winnings to buy her a new dress might be nice. The work clothes she wore now were fine but brown. Not that she looked drab, but something like her best dress in peach left her sparkling.

"Sure. You get your farm and I get my school. Maybe even on adjoining properties so we can visit each other as friends."

"You can make me coffee from now on."

Her face flushed pink and she glanced up from her plate. "It's good?"

"Very. Thank you," he said. She mumbled a 'you're welcome' to him and kept eating. Her breakfast smelled good but he knew better than to even have a taste. It was a long way to the outhouse for a sick man.

He sipped at his coffee, not wanting to overload

his stomach. She finished eating and began cleaning up the dishes. "I usually fill the washbasin in the evening," he offered.

She gave him a little grin while cleaning. "I wondered what your system was or if you even had one."

"I can do dishes before bed." Henry stood and poured a half cup of coffee.

"All right. You can show me and I can take over until I leave."

He went back to the bed and sat. The ham aroma lingered as he watched her tidy up the room. She moved with a fluid grace and he couldn't look away. Her hat was wedged between the dresser and her carpetbag, smashing the crown a little. The brim touching the floor might get dusty, too. "I can hang up your hat if you want."

She stopped dusting and turned to him with a smile. "There's no need to do so. It's fine where it is."

"No, really. I don't mind." He stood and the room spun. Sitting down to make the vertigo stop, he added, "Or, I'll let you when you're good and ready to."

"Thank you, but it truly is fine. I'll hang it up later." After another slight grin in his direction, Sally went back to dusting.

He watched as she paused at the window and looked out. The light coming in gave her a silhouette. Instead of yesterday's curl down her back, she had her hair in a long single braid. He rubbed his eyes before taking another sip. She appeared far more like a schoolmarm today and maybe even resembled a farmer's wife a little more, too.

Henry stopped watching her to stare ahead. They

were already married. His brother-in-law, Del, had offered to help him find a farm more than once. He didn't want to be beholden to anyone, yet, settling down with Sally did appeal to him. Heck, she'd be attractive to any man with eyes.

She walked in front of him and said, "I'm going outside to shake the dust and bring in water."

He glanced up to see her with the rag and pitcher. "All right. I'll let you."

"Stairs feel like too much of a challenge, hm?" she said with a chuckle. "Very well. I'm not sure what cures whiskey-itis except time and coffee. Maybe a greasy beef stew?"

With a groan, he covered his eyes with a hand. "No. Not that. Not anything to do with food or drink ever again." She laughed again as the door opened and closed. Alone in the room, he uncovered his eyes and smiled. Her amusement, even at his expense, left him feeling better than a hangover allowed. Plus, he'd even prefer thinking about his queasy stomach than how her lips felt yesterday.

She'd kissed him like a stranger at first. Not surprising, but as they remained together, she'd softened under him and he couldn't help but respond. He shivered. The blood rushed from his brain, leaving him dizzy again.

He drained the last of the coffee. In any other situation, he'd have spent his wedding night in bed with her and not at the pub with the boys. But then, she should have been honest in her abilities as a farmer's wife, too.

Henry went over to put the cup in with the other dishes. She might be able to keep a nice house but he needed a woman good with a plow. *Plus,* he thought and went to the window, he wanted a woman who could give him children. Sally might be able to carry a child to term, but give birth? No, he wanted someone who could have a baby in the morning and be ready to work in the afternoon.

His advertisement had been clear. He needed to remember that. Whatever had possessed Sally to think she'd make a good farmer's wife was her fault. Not his.

"Goodness!" The door closed behind her. "There are some colorful people living here." She gave him a quick smile before putting the water in its basin on the dresser. "Sorry for the delay. I hope you weren't thirsty. Your neighbors are friendly and asked a lot of questions."

Her appearance hit him in the gut again. Henry hated how much his heart raced every time she spoke. He hated her laugh. How it pleased him deep in his heart. And finally, he hated how much he wanted to make excuses for why he had to marry her. He wanted to give up every one of his dreams if doing so pleased her.

All of his work in the past ten years would be for nothing if he stopped saving for a farm. The freezing nights on the river with the unending stench of fish. Worse, the roasting days, again with fish in the hold. The smell permeated everything he wore. Days off weren't enjoyable any more. The following shift just meant getting used to the grind all over again. He stood and shook off the throbbing in his head.

"We're a quiet pair, aren't we?" She smoothed the blanket over their bed and fluffed the pillows. "You'd think we might have more to talk about today."

"I suppose," he muttered. Her happiness dug

under his skin like a swarm of chiggers.

"How are you feeling? Would you like more coffee? Or maybe tea?" Sally came over to him and put a hand on his forehead. "You feel normal."

"No, stop." He took a step back. "I don't need you doing things for me. I don't need you here, period, so stop being so nice."

"I'm sorry?"

Henry couldn't look at her. "I came home drunk last night and am hung over now. You should be furious with me and throwing things, stomping out, and going home. What's wrong with you? Why are you still here?"

Sally was quiet for a few moments. She folded the dust cloth before pulling out the chair and sitting at the tiny kitchen table. "I thought we had an agreement, a plan of sorts. We get married. You let me stay here in exchange for cooking and cleaning. I find a teaching position. We have our marriage annulled."

"I know." He rubbed his face. "I know. I'm just feeling the effects of last night, I suppose."

"Yes, you are, and *will* for the rest of the day." She began wiping the table.

"All right, look. Let's go to the dry goods store and see what all we'll need for later." He grabbed his boots and sat on the edge of the bed. "I waited to shop for anything since I knew you'd want to buy things you liked, too."

"Oh, I don't know." She stared at the ceiling. "I should probably stay here and keep busy. I don't really want to spend any money."

He paused in pulling on his second boot. "You don't want to *what*? I swear, lady. If you were a bit huskier, you'd be the perfect woman for me."

"Maybe we should go by the bakery, instead, and fatten me up so you'll like me a little more." She stood up and smoothed her skirt. "I might need to go with you, after all. Who else would make sure you buy more than cakes and pies for me."

Henry shrugged. Just because he planned on their annulment didn't mean he wanted her here alone all the time. "Sure. Come along and make sure I buy everything I need."

"Thank you. Let me grab my things."

He waited until she put on her bonnet and grabbed her carpetbag. "Will you need those?"

"I will. We can carry our purchases in this." She held up the bag. "And I need something to protect me from the sun."

"Very well. Let's go." He got up and held the door open for her. She waited until he locked up before following him downstairs. "We don't have far to go. I'd hire a buggy but would rather save the money."

"So would I."

Sally thinking about saving him money pleased him. Although, her wanting to bulk up to stay his wife didn't sit on his mind. The woman was perfect the way she was and didn't need to change. She couldn't help it if she weren't farm wife material. He'd be just as unhappy if he'd wanted a dainty schoolteacher but received a husky girl instead.

He glanced over at her as she looked around at Portland. Wonder and curiosity shown from her expression. Marrying a smart woman would have its advantages. He looked in the same directions she did, trying to see the city through her eyes. All he saw was a lot of the same.

"Henry?"

He turned at the familiar voice to see an old family friend. "Mr. Granville. It's a pleasure to see you."

"Same here." He grinned and looked from Henry to Sally. "Hello, ma'am. Don't tell me you're walking with this varmint."

"I am," she said. "I'm Sally Du—"

"She's Miss Sally Wigg, from back east," Henry interjected and frowned at her to go along with the charade. "You know, one of my war buddy's sisters out here for a visit."

"Oregon is very lucky to be your vacation spot, ma'am." Sam tipped his hat at her.

"Thank you, Mr. Granville. I feel fortunate to be here."

"It's Sam, please." He turned to Henry. "It's good seeing you today. I'll tell the wife you said hello because I'm sure she'll send her love."

He grinned. Marie Granville was the kindest woman he'd ever met. She helped care for him and his younger brother when their sister went missing and their pa died. "Good. Send her mine as well. It's been too long."

"I agree. Stop by the house sometime and stay for dinner." He smiled at Sally. "Soon, before this little lady returns east. We'll want to have you both over for a visit."

"Will do."

"A pleasure meeting you, miss. Unfortunately, I need to continue on home. Marie will have my hide if I'm not there for lunch."

"Same here," Sally said with a smile. She turned to Henry, her grin fading the further Sam walked away. "Shall we continue?"

Henry held out his arm for her to take. "Yes."

"I'm fine, thank you," she said and began walking.

He caught up after a few steps. "Do you know where you're going?"

"I figured I'd walk until reaching the store or the ocean. Whichever was first."

After a chuckle, he went with her for a while, both of them silent. "Mr. Granville and his crew were the guides who led us from Missouri to here, back when I was young. My mother and father died along the way."

"I'm sorry to hear that."

Her softened voice warmed his heart. He hadn't wanted to tell her his life story but the words came tumbling out. "My sister and her husband raised me and my younger brother, Buster."

"You're lucky to have family able to take you in."

"I am." He stopped when she did and realized why when seeing the dry goods sign above the door. "This is where I usually go."

She glanced from the store to him with a slight smile. "I guessed as much."

He grinned and held the door open for her. "Go on, smarty." She walked in and he wondered what she thought about the place. "I suppose this is a little rougher than your city stores."

"A little. Less stone and more wood than home, but I like it." She walked on, nodding to the storekeeper as Henry trailed behind her. "Everything here seems so much cleaner. I enjoy the fresher air, too."

He watched as she read the various labels for the shelved jars. "Back east has a lot of good qualities, but you're right. I love Oregon. It's always been my home, no matter how far I go."

She looked at him for a moment before resuming her shopping. "I noticed your bookmark in the Atlas. Is that a wish list or a completed one?"

"Mostly wish." He went to stand beside her. "I've been to some of the places. Nothing in Europe or Asia, though."

"Hmm." She went on and stopped at the coffee bean barrel. "We need more."

He shrugged. She'd know better than he would. "We probably need a little of everything."

Sally filled a paper bag with a couple of scoops. "I don't want to buy a lot just for me. Not when I'm leaving eventually."

She had a point. No sense in purchasing for two when one would be moving on soon. He could say so but figured she already accepted the inevitable. "Get as much as you want. Almost everything will keep for a while."

A shadow passed over her face as she fastened the bag so the beans wouldn't spill. She gave him the coffee and said, "Sometimes, like at our wedding when we kissed, I forget this is all a sham. I have the urge to make our marriage a happy one." She took a few steps forward, bending to read the barrels' labels. "Ridiculous, isn't it? Especially when you've been quite clear you don't care for me at all."

Henry couldn't agree. He did like her. No, he *adored* her. If he were willing to throw away his dream of a peaceful country life surrounded by a large family, he'd stay married to her. "I'm sorry. I know changing my mind after you arrived was bad. It hurt your feelings but our annulment will be for the best."

He waited a few seconds, watching for any hint of

a reaction as she stared at the flour barrel. "You deserve a banker or business man for a husband, not some former sailor turned farmer."

She turned to him while getting another paper bag. "I'm beginning to agree with you."

CHAPTER SIX

Sally gave him the full bag of flour to hold before she went on to the sugar and salt barrels. Henry had seemed surprised at first about her directness. Too bad. His constant reminder of how much he didn't want her dug at her like a splinter in her finger.

"Is this all we need?"

She turned to him. He held a small bag of flour along with coffee, soap, and a bag of rice. "I think so. The store is close enough to your home that I can come here on my own if necessary."

He began to say something before closing his mouth and nodding. "Then I'll go pay for everything."

Before she could say anything, he was headed toward the counter. She bit her lip. If she offered to pay, she'd have to take money from her bonnet. He'd know about her secret savings. He'd be furious over her keeping quiet about the funds and marrying him anyway. Maybe as angry as she was when he pretended she wasn't his wife to his friend earlier.

She walked along to the housewares section. His

distance with Mr. Granville made sense to her, logically, even if it stung emotionally. Henry had been honest about refusing to stay married. Besides, she didn't want a man who could get stumbling drunk when out with friends.

Sally shivered. At least he had only been intoxicated. She'd been sheltered in the Home, still, she'd seen drunks of all kinds everywhere else but at Madam Wiggie's.

The door's bell clanged and she glanced over at the cash register to see if Henry had finished paying, yet. The clerk rang up the customer. Only, the person wasn't Henry. She frowned and went up to the counter, looking everywhere else for her pretend husband.

"Are you looking for the man you walked in with, ma'am?"

She smiled at the friendly faced shopkeeper. "Yes, I am. Did he pay and leave already?"

"Sure did."

"Thank you," she said and hurried out of the door. Was that Henry under a black hat just up the way? Sally couldn't be sure. Still, she knew his apartment was in the same direction so she hurried toward him. The man turned off to the right, down a street she'd never been on before, so he couldn't be Henry.

Every house and storefront looked the same to her, too new, too false, and too unknown. She walked on, keeping watch for anything familiar. A sapling here, a hitching post there reassured her as she continued toward where she hoped was her home. His home, she corrected herself. The inconsiderate jackass who-forgot-his-wife-in-the-store's home, not hers.

She took a deep breath, almost too angry to breathe. Maybe other men forgot their wives on the second day of their marriage, too. Men who didn't want to marry the woman, of course. Men who...her nose stung. Men who maybe liked the gal but couldn't love her. Henry had an interest in her in the first seconds they'd met, but not after. All because of what she looked like.

He didn't know the real strength of a woman at all. He couldn't know how hard she'd worked to save up funds for her own school. Most of the money hiding in her bonnet came from backbreaking work in a laundry. Madam Wiggie had helped, certainly. She put a hand on her bonnet for a couple of seconds. Everything else resulted from her own efforts.

"Hey, Ma'am, you missing a husband?"

She frowned at Henry's voice and saw him walking toward her. His smile screeched across her nerves like a hard-braking train. She'd been left behind for the second time since they'd met and not feeling kindly about him at all. "Was this a test?" she hissed. "To see if I could find my way back without mishap? Or were you hoping for something horrible to happen so you could free yourself of me?"

His jaw dropped before he recovered. "What? No, nothing of the sort." He opened the building door for her. "I wouldn't ever want you to be harmed. I just figured I could go home, drop off our purchases, and come back for you."

She didn't reply or continue the argument as they went up the stairs to his place. A large part of her wanted to believe him and his lack of malice. When they neared a landing, she asked, "So there was no ill intention in abandoning me in the store."

He stopped on the last stair so suddenly, she bumped into him. He turned and caught her, looking into her eyes. "Honestly, Sally, I meant nothing by either time. Distraction was the first reason and the second was I thought I'd be faster in coming back for you." He kissed her forehead and resumed the climb to the apartment.

A little more mollified by his surprise kiss, she couldn't help but let the anger go. "I suppose if I'd been less panicked, I might have remembered your address, since I wrote it in my journal."

He unlocked their door and held it open for her. "Which you left here."

"I did." She went over to the dresser and her things. "Serves me right for becoming comfortable so soon." She opened the drawer and her carpetbag and began packing.

"You don't have to do that. I'm sorry." He walked over to her to put a hand on her shoulder. "Really, I am. Next time, I'll tell you before running off."

The shamed face he wore convinced her he'd meant no harm. She leaned into his touch. "I'd appreciate your doing so. At least until I'm more familiar with the city." She double-checked the drawer to make sure she'd left nothing behind. "Now, would you like something to eat?"

"Yeah, I am getting a little hungry. I can help while you cook." He removed his hat and untied hers at the same time.

She froze. He went to the door while talking about what his favorite meals were. She didn't listen as he hung her hat next to his on the peg. Her heart started beating again when he came back over to her. She struggled to return his smile at first. "All right. I can make biscuits and beans for dinner."

"You'll need the cookpot." He went to pick up the small washtub of dishes. "I'll clean these up and be right back."

"All right." She watched as he went out. A breeze from the closing door caused the hats to lift a little. She sighed and leaned against the pantry dresser. He'd almost discovered her money. She really needed a better hiding place but other than sewing the bills into her hems, nothing seemed safe enough. After he went to work, she had to visit the bank and open an account.

Except, no. She was married now and everything hers was also his, legally. The hat would have to do until she could invest in her new school. She would just have to sew an extra lining to hide her money and be careful until then.

Full of nervous energy now, she glanced around the room. Dishwashing would take him a while. She could have the bed made and the floor swept by the time he returned. The broom was in plain sight in a corner near the door, and he stored his rags in the bottom drawer of the pantry dresser.

The air seemed stuffy so she opened the window a bit. A warm pine smell drifted in so she pushed open the sash a little more. She enjoyed the breeze for a moment before building up the stove's fire for their meal. She finished up and looked around the room, satisfied with her work.

Henry came in with the clean dishes. "I was thinking we could visit the wharf and buy some fish if you'd like. Or I could bring home a can or two of salmon after work."

"Both ideas sound nice, thank you." She took the

cookpot from him and placed it on the stove. "How often do you visit the store?"

He shrugged out of his jacket and hung it up. "I don't know. As often as I need to, I guess."

"Hmm." She opened the drawer where Henry kept the potatoes and onions together. "I hope you don't mind, but we need to find separate places for these."

"Go ahead. I know Sis keeps them apart in the root cellar." The bed squeaked when he sat and began pulling off his boots.

"She's smart." Sally rearranged the dresser until she'd put the two onions in the top drawer and moved the potatoes to the very bottom. "This will have to do until you get a potato bin."

He came over to stand beside her. "Seems like a lot of trouble for just me."

She stopped while peeling a couple of potatoes for their dinner. "You're right. It probably is, but worth the effort. Otherwise, do as you please."

"No, you're right." Henry took out his pocketknife and began peeling the other potato. "I never thought to do in the kitchen what I'd do on the farm."

"It's why your potatoes are trying to grow." She gave him a quick smile before cutting a quarter from the onion. "They'll last longer if you keep them apart."

He chuckled and gave her the finished potato. "I just thought I had a way with plants."

"You probably do, or should have a way with them, considering your life's ambition." She mixed the vegetables together with a little flour, salt, and pepper.

"So, I suppose you have a way with children?"

Sally dropped a teaspoon of lard in the heated

frying pan. "I'd like to think so."

He leaned against the dresser and looked at her. "Have you ever taught before?"

"I have, actually." She gave him a smile and sprinkled the chopped mixture into the pan. "At the Home when I was old enough. All of us girls, A to Z, are schoolteachers now."

"All of you? Were there a lot of students in your school?"

"Yes." She stirred the food. "Madam Wiggie took us in when we were babies or very young, in some cases. As we came in, she gave us an alphabetical name. I was 'S' and received Sally—well, Sarah at first until Sally stuck."

"It's a pretty name."

"Thank you. It's mine and I happen to like it." The food sizzled in the pan for a little while until she asked," How about you, Henry Jackson DuBoise? Care to tell me more about yourself?"

"We've written a lot more about our plans for the future than what happened in our past, haven't we?" He pulled up a chair from the table and sat.

She smiled at him while putting the cooked potatoes on his plate. "At least we agree on where our focus is."

"I wasn't always Henry," he said. "Everyone called me Skeeter for the longest time. After I enlisted near the end of the war, I changed it to Henry."

Sally set his plate in front of him and began filling her bowl. "Did everyone stop calling you Skeeter then?" She joined him at the table.

He nodded and wiped his mouth. "Eventually. I can tell how long I've known a person by what they call me. Before the end of the war, I'm Skeeter. After?

I'm Henry."

She paused eating. "And DuBoise? Are you French?" His expression saddened and she regretted asking the question.

"No. My sister married a French Indian and he adopted us boys."

Sally would bet anything there was an interesting, unspoken story. She wanted to know more and asked, "You mentioned a younger brother in your letters." She hoped talking about his siblings would cheer him a little.

He chuckled and put down his fork. "Yes, Buster. Or Bert as he likes to be known as now."

"Ah ha, a name change like you did." She took his plate to the stove and gave him more dinner.

"Yep. He's a smaller version of me, as my sister says."

She set the food in front of him and continued her meal. "Bet he's a handful."

He swallowed. "He is. He's studying to be a lawyer like Del, our brother-in-law."

Henry's life choices fascinated her. He seemed so certain of his future yet his past didn't seem to follow a straight line to where he wanted to go. She ate for a little while before saying, "But you're the sailor and farmer?"

He took a bite and chewed. "I am. More of a bargeman than a sailor anymore."

"From your description in the *Bulletin*, I thought you were always on the high seas," she said. "Did you ever sail to faraway places?"

"Never as much as I wanted to. During the war. I enlisted to be on the ships to see the world." He stabbed a chunk of potato. "I saw a lot more than I bargained for."

Sally had been born three years before the war started, but her history studies included recent events. She wanted to hug him but didn't know if he'd welcome the gesture. "Most people did. Such a tragedy for us all."

"It's also water under the bridge and out to sea." He pushed his plate forward. "Excellent meal. I'm glad we're married."

Her face heated from the praise and the twinkle in his eyes. "Thank you." She ate her last few bites. "Tomorrow night, I'll cook whatever fish you bring home, if you'd like."

"I would like that a lot." He stared at the empty plate for a few seconds. "I am sorry about leaving you behind today. Abandoning you wasn't my intent. I thought I'd be helping in case you wanted to shop more."

She stood and took both his plate and her bowl to the washtub. "Thank you, and I might have. Of course, paying attention to where you were might have been good for me, too."

He chuckled. "For both of us. I suppose I need to get used to having a wife. Especially if an annulment is harder than I think it'll be."

Sally sat back down and propped her chin on her palm with an elbow on the table. "I think finding a schoolteacher job will be more difficult. I'm relying on you to tell me where all of the schools are."

"I'm aware of the one I went to in Oregon City." He shrugged. "I'm sure there are plenty around here and close by, too. Portland and the surrounding area has done nothing but grown in the past twenty years."

"Could you make me a list of the ones you suspect

are nearby? You might have seen them while going to work or visiting someone."

"I know a few, sure. There's P—"

"Wait." She hopped up and went to her carpetbag. "I'll have you write down what you remember." She opened up to a blank back page and set the journal with its pencil on the table in front of him.

He scratched his chin while looking at her and the taller dresser. "I reckon you could unpack after all. I won't be leaving you behind again."

Sally studied him for a few moments to guess his mood. He seemed a little embarrassed but honest. The lost feeling, while in a strange city, hadn't left her from earlier, though. Not that she wanted to grind his face into the mistake, but she didn't feel safe enough just yet. "Thank you. I might take the time later to do so. Right now, I have a few dishes to rinse." Before he could argue, she added, "You might list your favorite foods and dinners as well. I don't expect to get a job right away and it'll help me to know your preferences before I leave."

Henry glanced up from his scribbles with a grin. "Careful there, I might not want an annulment if you feed me too well."

She stopped putting silverware into the pan for cleaning to look at him. "*You* be careful or I'll start thinking you don't hate me too much."

"I don't hate you. Not at all," he said with a frown and stared down at the list. "Problem is, I like you too much."

"Hmm." Her hand shook a little as she put the frying pan in last. "I might have the same problem in liking you too much, too." She sighed and put a bright smile on her face. "Such a quandary, isn't it?

Two married people who aren't fighting. Imagine that." She picked up the washtub and retrieved the soap from the shelf near the stove. "If you'll excuse me."

Sally escaped the room before tears filled her eyes. She blinked them back and went down the staircase to the water pump behind the building. People wandered around doing their various tasks. The door shut hard behind her, with the metal fixtures clanging. The pump sat a little ways from the back porch. A horse trough caught the water underneath the spigot and she shook her head. Someone had left suds in the tank.

Thinking of how the horses might become sick from lye soap, she gave the handle a few pumps. The suds flowed over the far side and onto the hard ground. Various men looked at her but none stopped to protest her actions. Satisfied the animals' water flowed clear enough, she filled the frying pan with water. She balanced the pan on the trough rim and began cleaning everything.

"Hey, little lady."

She glanced up to see a large man standing across from her. The trough separated them. Still, considering the gleam in his eyes, she didn't feel safe. "Good afternoon."

"You're doing a fine job of washing. A pretty gal like you shouldn't have to be someone's maid." He balanced his bulk on the edge of the water tank. "Unless you're married. You're too fancy to be married to anyone living here."

"I'm marr…not. Not married." She bit her lip over how close she'd come to claiming Henry as her husband. He always denied their relationship with people he knew and this man might be a friend of his. She needed to help out her temporary husband by not spilling any beans. "I mean, I just come in and tidy up a place for a customer or two. Extra money."

"Really?" He sat up from his slouch. "I wouldn't mind a lady coming over to my home once in a while. I'd even pay her for the privilege." He trailed his fingertips in the water. "Do you have a set fee for the services you offer?"

Sally didn't doubt his meaning was a lot more salacious than his words indicated. She wanted to grab the dishes and run back to Henry's apartment. But if she did, this man might be waiting for her the next time she needed water. She'd never find a moment's peace if he lived in the apartment complex, too. "I only have one client in this building and can't take on any new customers. It's temporary until I find more permanent employment."

"Employment, huh?" The man grinned and showed spaces where teeth should have been. "You sure are a posh one. From back east, aren't ya?" He stood, stretching out his legs. "I'd like to find a permanent place for fancy city gal like you." He came over to her, his smell following him. "Somewhere real close to me, if you're interested."

She held the dishes close to her torso like a shield. "Sorry, I can't be interested at all. It's a shame, because you're a nice man and all." She took a step back toward the porch. "I'm not the kind of woman you'd want to hire and I'm sure a man like you could do better."

"Aw, don't say that." He sauntered up to her. "You're pretty and, if you're interested in some quick cash, we could make some sort of arrangement."

"Sorry, I like slow cash and need to get back to work." She hurried up the stairs to the back door. "Nice meeting you and good day." Not waiting for his reply, she hiked her skirt and rushed to the apartment.

Mercifully, Henry had left the door unlocked. He looked up when she rushed in and frowned. "You look like a ghost is on your tail."

He didn't need to know what had happened. She didn't want him blaming her for causing trouble in the building. Thinking quick she blurted out, "I think I saw a mouse."

He laughed. "Is that all? I figured you'd be tougher than that." He stood and yawned before adding, "I wrote down a lot of dinners I like. You don't have to cook all of them. I just wanted to make sure you had plenty to pick from when deciding on meals."

She set the dishes down on the warm stove to help dry them. Clasping her shaking hands, she went over and read his list. Most of what he'd written were foods she liked as well. Which was good for her since she'd been known to go to bed hungry to avoid eating anything repulsive. "Thank you. This will be extremely helpful."

"Are you sure you're fine?" He went over to her, his clear blue eyes searching hers. "If I didn't know better, I'd say something more than a mouse spooked you."

Sally couldn't meet his gaze or he'd know she was lying. "No, just the mouse. Or what I thought was one." She went over to the window. "At any rate, it's becoming a little chillier in here. Should I close the window?"

"Yeah, and I'll stoke the fire for us, too."

She closed and locked the window. Gaslights came on throughout the town, each a small protest against the darkening twilight. Henry didn't know her well enough to see through her lie. She'd seen rats far bigger than any mouse—as recently as last month. Rodents didn't bother her as much as the human-rat at the water trough had.

She glanced up to see Henry's reflection in the window glass. He was still frowning at her and she wanted to distract him. "Portland is a beautiful city."

"It is."

She nodded at his makeshift nightstand. "Have you read your copy of *Tom Sawyer*, yet?"

"I have." He went over and retrieved the book from the middle of the stack. "How about you?"

"I'd like to." She took the offered novel from him. "I've read Twain's work in the newspaper. He's one of my favorites."

"Mine, too." Henry pulled out *The Steam Powered Man*. "I'll light an extra lamp for the both of us."

"Thank you." She tapped the spine of the book against her hand as he locked the door and lit two lamps for them. When he settled onto one of the dining chairs, she did, too. "Is this your first time reading that particular book?"

"Yes. I'd bought it a couple of weeks ago but have been too busy getting ready for a guest." He grinned at her. "Seems like cleaning up a place, getting an extra chair, and a bigger bed eats up a lot of a man's free time."

She smiled. "It's appreciated. Maybe since his guest is here to help him, the man can now catch up on his reading after a good meal."

Henry opened the book, his face red. "I reckon the

man is mighty grateful to have his guest here after all."

CHAPTER SEVEN

Henry opened his eyes to the dark room. His job on the cannery boats began at dawn. Judging from the pitch black outside, he had plenty of time to get ready and go.

He turned over, still surprised Sally lived with him. They might have had a few weeks to get used to the idea of marriage before she arrived, but reality was different.

Now, Henry had a wife he couldn't—no, he wouldn't—love. He glanced over at her. Too little light existed to see her despite her soft snores telling him where she was. He closed his eyes. God help him, he even loved her breathing. Yesterday had been such a fiasco and he wouldn't live long enough to make up for leaving her behind at the store. He'd overestimated how deep into a daydream she'd been in.

Henry eased his way out of bed. He had nothing else to do but work hard and…what? Prove he loved her? Prove he didn't mean to abandon her? Prove he'd be a better husband?

He stood and shook his head. No. He needed to prove nothing to a wife who deserved better. They both knew she wasn't cut out to be a farmhand/wife to him. She was sunshine filled music rooms with charming and clean children, shared with her banker husband. All he could plan to give her was a roughhewn home with children like he'd been. And that was if she were lucky.

An unlucky woman would be like his Ma and marry someone like his Pa. Henry snorted while pulling on a boot. He might rethink this whole farm wife thing and just hire help. Plenty of children needed adopting, too.

Heck, Sally and all of her sisters were orphans at one time. He wouldn't mind having a houseful of boys to take fishing and help out on the farm. Girls were nice, women were nicer most of the time, but he didn't think adopted daughters would like to skip rocks, climb trees, hunt, and race horses for fun.

The ghostly gray of predawn light eased across the apartment. Henry sighed and grabbed his coat, dislodging Sally's bonnet in the process. He replaced her hat on its hook and gave her one last look before leaving for work.

Like the last item remaining on a to do list, Sally stayed on his mind all day. He did the usual work of pulling the nets on board, dumping salmon into the hold, and replacing the nets for later. Then, a run to the cannery in Astoria when the boat filled. Repeat until sundown, sleep, and back at it the next day.

Henry stepped off of the boat aware of his smell. He couldn't let Sally wash his fishy clothes. Yet another reason to find her a job and let her move on with her life.

"Hey, DuBoise, can you hold one for a minute?"

A little tremor of dread went through him from his boss's voice. His quotas had all been met or exceeded, Henry reassured his worry. He lifted his chin and asked, "Sure, Skipper, what do you need?"

The tubby man in coveralls walked up to him. "Our main office sent a letter wanting our best man for their newest boat. I thought of you right away, if you're interested."

Henry took the letter and read it. He'd get more money but would need to move. "Sacramento? I'm not sure I'd want to live there."

Skipper peered over the top of the letter. "For nearly double the money, I'd move to the Antarctic."

He looked over the letter again with a smile as an answer to his boss. Moving meant leaving Sally, unless she moved with him. "I'd like to talk it over with someone, first."

"Sure. You need time to make a decision. Just don't wait too long or the boys will find someone else."

He nodded. "Will do." A little numb from the potential raise in pay, he crossed the street and headed home. The letter felt alive in his pocket. His first impulse was to pack up tonight and be in Sacramento by the morning. Except, he wanted Sally to go with him.

Henry sighed and scratched his chin. Maybe a couple of years as his wife in another town would toughen her up for farm life. He couldn't help but smile at the idea of staying married to her. Every minute they were together flew by as fast and the minutes apart dragged.

Once at the apartment complex, he hurried in and

took the stairs two at a time. He fished in his pocket for the key before remembering he'd slid it under the door for her. He knocked a couple of times and waited until she answered the door.

Sally peeked out before pulling the door wide. "Oh good, it's you. Welcome back. Dinner is ready when you are, but no rush."

The warm room and heavenly cooking hit him hard. "I'm starved and could get used to a life like this."

"What?" She chuckled. "Are you saying I might not be the worst wife in the world after all?" She set a full bowl with a spoon in front of his chair. "Did you hit your head at work today, dearest?"

Henry grinned while taking off his jacket and hat. "No, though I did get a letter from headquarters." He found his seat. "A complete surprise."

"Oh?" She sat, her chin resting on her hand. "A good one, I hope."

"I think so." He took a bite of the beans. The taste overshadowed whatever he wanted to say. "I didn't know we had ham," he managed to say after swallowing.

"We didn't. I have a little bit of a fund and went to the butcher's today. We also needed more potatoes."

"I'll give you some money."

She waved a hand. "Don't worry about it. You paid for everything yesterday. I could help today." She put her spoon on the table. "So? What's your surprise, or can I not hear?"

"Yeah," he said and dug around in his pocket. "I have a chance for a promotion." He nodded when she raised her eyebrows. "Go ahead. I think you'll like the amount."

Sally scanned the letter, a "Goodness gracious!" slipping out when seeing his new salary.

He grinned, happy to have impressed her. "See? I knew you'd be surprised."

"I am." She folded the letter and slid it over to him. "You'll take the job, of course."

"I want to, but I'd rather stay here."

"Here? Hmm." She stood and poured water for both of them. "I don't know. That's a fine salary to turn down."

"I agree." He ate the last bite of ham and beans. "So if I take the job and move, what would you want to do?"

She sat with her cup and gave him a smile. "Well, I managed to meet with the county superintendent today."

Henry didn't quite know what to feel. If she found work here, she'd probably not move to Sacramento with him. He put the spoon in his bowl. "How did that go for you?"

"He's coming here, day after tomorrow, to interview me for a teacher's position. The school is within walking distance, even in bad weather."

Her excited expression added to her happy voice. She really wanted this chance and when he took the Sacramento job, she'd have to scramble for another place to live. "Does the superintendent know you're married?"

Sally's smile faded and she bit her lip before replying, "No, he thinks I'm single. It was one of the requirements for the job." She stood and refreshed his water. "I figured you'd be happy with my denial of you in public. I'll just need you to stay gone the day after tomorrow."

He wasn't happy with her denial at all but didn't have the time right now to dwell on why. As for her needing him to not be home for a while, he could do so easily. "Won't be difficult. I'll be at work then."

"Good, and thank you." She sighed and put his empty bowl in the washbasin. "Now, if I could convince our landlord to let a single woman rent here, I'd be happy."

Hearing her say she'd enjoy not being married to him left Henry feeling like he was hungover on the inside. He didn't want to leave, but didn't want to lose her altogether. "We could stay married while I'm gone."

"Except, my job requirement." She put her elbows on the table and rested her chin on her hands. "I can't be married and I can't be single. Not if I want to work and have a home."

An idea hit him, but he didn't know if she'd be agreeable. So many of the men he'd served with at the end of the Civil War had died. By cannon fire, buckshot, or drowning, they'd left loved ones behind. Sally wasn't old enough, yet the idea could work to her benefit. "How about you're a widow after I leave? I move south, work hard, save my money, and then when I'm ready to buy my farm, we can get our annulment."

She sat up with a smile. "Your idea does seem to solve our problems. Although...." She stared out at the city a few seconds before asking, "Do you have an estimate of how long you'd be gone?"

He figured how much he had versus how much he wanted to spend on land. "I'd like to save up another couple thousand dollars."

Sally gave him a quick look. "Two thousand?" He

nodded and she bit her lip for a moment. "What if you had a gift of a thousand and borrowed the remaining amount to buy your farm? Would that be enough to help you find your dream and to keep you in Portland?"

He laughed at the amount. "I guess so, except what sort of person would give me so much money?"

She stood and went over to her bonnet hanging on the wall. "Probably someone who cares enough about you to help make your dream come true."

Henry's heart began thumping in his chest. Her words were exactly what he never wanted to hear. Things were bad enough now that he'd fallen for her and had second thoughts about the annulment. The marriage was supposed to be a sham and now she talked like he mattered to her, too? Dinner jumped around in his stomach and his mouth watered. He couldn't let any of this continue or they'd be madly in love with each other like his mother had said his father had been with her.

She came back with her hat, sat opposite from him, and turned her bonnet upside down. "You see, when we first met, you assumed I was a weak and helpless woman." She began pulling a liner from the crown of her hat. "I'm not." Returning to her efforts, she smiled and said, "I've worked hard as a laundress for my money." She set the liner aside. "Lye, hot water, stirring until I thought my arms would fall off, and hot summer days without end all brought me a tidy sum."

Henry blinked as she pulled money from the hidden compartment. He counted the bills silently as she retrieved each one. "You've been carrying around a thousand dollars this entire time?"

"For the most part." She stacked the money on the table in front of him. "It's yours if you'll stay here, buy your farm, and let me start a school on a small part of the land. We can be man and wife. If you'd prefer to not live as a married couple fully, I'm sure separate bedrooms are possible. I would like to have babies someday, though, and well...." She looked down at the table. "I might not mind your help. You're my husband and the handsomest man I know."

The reality of the money, and her words, swirled in his head. He didn't even want to address their children. She'd lied by omission to him since they'd met. "You had money?" he croaked. "Yet, you insisted I marry you."

She quickly looked up at him and said, "Not *insist*, really, but more like suggested."

He stood, his chair falling back behind him. The noise made Sally jump but he couldn't pay attention right now. "You could have found any room in Portland with this much cash." Anger and hurt crashed into him as if he were a rowboat in a hurricane. "You've lied to me from the start. First about being a good farm wife, then about not being able to afford anything." He ran a hand through his hair, frustrated and more than furious with her. "I don't know what to do with you."

She also stood. "You could stay married to me, take the money, buy our farm, and let me prove to you I'm as strong as any other woman you'd find out there." Leaning forward to put her hands on the table, she continued. "That's what you could do. In fact, that's what any sane man would do, even if he hated me. He'd want the chance to reach his long term goal."

He looked at her, really focused on her face, her beautiful, expressive, and affectionate face. She matched him in every way, and he couldn't help but adore her. He shook his head. "I don't hate you, not at all. I just want honesty from you."

"Thank you. I don't hate you, either, and agree you deserved to know before now." She pushed in her chair and walked around the table to him. "I wanted to tell you but also wanted a chance to prove I'd be a good wife to you."

Tendrils of dark hair framed her face. A glisten of sweat beaded her brow from her efforts in fixing him dinner. Henry wanted to believe she was right. That she'd make a great wife to him and the best mother to all the children he wanted. She made him wish he were a better man with loftier goals. Yet, all he'd ever wanted to do since the war was live off of the land in a quiet place of his own. He cleared his throat and said, "Any man would be lucky to have you, Sally. I know I am, even if I don't deserve you, but I can't let you work a plow or feed hogs...."

"Does this mean you'll at least consider keeping me?"

Her eyes were all warm and sparkly. Just like when his sister looked at her husband. Sally had worked hard, yet was willing to give her money so his dream could come true? Heck, he'd thought his dream came true when she answered his advertisement. And yet, no, he couldn't stay married to such a delicate beauty. He had to be strong and give her up for her own good. "You can stay here until the end of the month when the lease is finished. After that, you'll need to find somewhere else to live."

Her slight smile faded. She stared down at the floor and softly said, "I understand."

CHAPTER EIGHT

Sally refused to sniff. All the tears in her could fall over the bridge of her nose to her temple. No sniffles or wiping nose. She turned over on her back. Henry might be gone for the day but that didn't mean she could give into self-pity.

No. Instead, she'd focus on tomorrow, when Mr. Bromley visited her. He'd make sure she wasn't married. Much easier now, since Henry planned to leave.

Unseeing in the inky darkness, she went over Madam Wiggie's interview instructions. Only, all she could think about was the hurt and disappointment on Henry's face last night. She'd confessed about the money, at least. He'd had that cold anger about him for the rest of the evening. The same as when she'd helped Uma put a frog in Rebecca's bed. At least Tillie had laughed, too.

She threw back the covers. Never mind Henry. He'd cool off and think about what he wanted in life. Then he'd realize she was his answer.

The stove was warm when she touched it and the

coffee still hot. She smiled. He may not want to be married to her but he was still considerate. She poured a cup and sat. The early golden sunlight reflected into the room and gave everything a glow.

Once her cup was empty, she began tidying up the apartment. Mr. Bromley would be arriving tomorrow morning. She would want to wash, dry, and iron her Sunday dress today. Considering she'd already read several of Henry's books, she liked the idea of a fall cleaning keeping her busy until the interview.

She looked at the wash pan and then the door. Henry arrived home so late. She couldn't ask him to do the dishes or the laundry. Yet, she didn't feel safe doing anything but dart to the outhouse and back. The odious man she'd met had to work sometime. She would just have to keep a note of when he lurked around and when the area was safe.

Sally hurried out into a drizzly day with a pail and washtub to fill with water. Making one trip to the pump was tough but helpful in avoiding lewd comments from her new "friend." She balanced the tub on a hip while unlocking the door. The heavy pail dug into her palm until she placed the container on the stove.

Soon, she'd eaten a cold lunch and began scrubbing her dress. Henry didn't have a clothesline of any sort. She improvised and used the back of a chair. The frying pan caught the dripping water as she began washing and rinsing the sheets. Henry would appreciate the freshness, she hoped.

The two pillows side by side stopped her for a moment. Mr. Bromley probably wasn't going to inspect their bed to make sure she wasn't married. Would he?

She looked around the apartment. Did anything say married couple or single woman lying about a man living with her? Nothing jumped out at her, but then, nothing said young woman on her own. She might need to prop up her journal on the dresser. Emptying her bag and scattering her belongings would add to the illusion.

Sally went back to wringing out the sheets. She could swear that, sometimes, Henry seemed irritated when they talked about an annulment. If she didn't know any better, she'd say he was afraid. Except, he'd written to her about his war experiences while running supplies. The man had been nothing but brave amidst so much danger.

She hung up the last dripping hand towel. Nothing she felt for him mattered, anyway. None of his reasons, none of the money she'd neglected to mention, and she supposed the kiss didn't matter as much to him, either. He didn't want her here and she shouldn't want to stay with him anymore.

Later in the afternoon, she took the chance to write in her journal. Not anything about the man at the water trough, of course, but updating her list. Tomorrow, she'd be able to cross off employment. A knock at the door startled her. She glanced outside to check the time. The caller couldn't be Henry home so soon. She stood up and went to the door. "Yes?"

"Miss Wigg?"

She recognized his voice and oh dear God, it was Mr. Bromley. "Yes, Mr. Bromley?"

"I was in your neighborhood and decided to move up our interview time, if you're willing."

She leaned against the door as if to keep him out with her weight. "Certainly." She bit her lip to keep from adding, "not." After a deep breath, she realized now was the best time to let the interview begin, show him her home, and let him leave before Henry came back.

She opened the door for him. "It's a pleasure to see you. Do come in." He walked into the apartment and she added, "I've been cleaning, getting ready for tomorrow." She made a sweeping gesture over her dress and tucked her hair into her bun. "Including myself."

"You have a very nice place." He took off his top hat, letting her take it to hang on a peg. "Very nice. Do you live here alone?"

"Sadly, yes. I had a roommate until she married." Sally removed her drying dress and sheets from the chairs, rolling them up before placing them in the wash tub. They'd just have to dry later. She worked fast to wipe down the chairs for him no matter which one he chose.

He tilted his head sideways at Henry's book where it lay on the makeshift nightstand. "*The Steam Powered Man*. Hmm, do you like that particular novel?"

To lie or not? She was rubbish with falsehoods so went for the truest statement. "I haven't read that particular story. It was one my brother recommended."

"One of my newest favorites." He picked up and opened the book where Henry had left a slip of paper. "Hmm, this must be your brother's, too."

"It probably is." She set a coffee cup on the table. "May I get you something to drink? Coffee, perhaps?"

"Water, please." He pulled out a chair and sat. "I'd like to get started, if you don't mind."

She nodded. Her hand didn't shake as she poured

him a drink. "Let me get my journal and I'll be ready," she said and froze. Her notes were in her carpetbag as if she were a guest here. Which she was, but Mr. Bromley could not know that. "One moment."

Sally hurried to her bag, retrieving her book and pencil. A step at a time, she thought, and took a deep breath while her back was turned to him. "I keep my book in my larger bag." She turned around and sat at the table with him. "A person never knows when inspiration will strike."

"Indeed." He smiled at her. "I have several questions for you. Each will give me an idea of your abilities and habits. Shall we begin?"

"Yes, please." She placed her hands on the table.

"Very well. Tell me about your childhood and home life." He interlaced his fingers. "We like to know if a teacher has a solid upbringing."

"I see." Madam Wiggie never mentioned how the education system would view orphan girls as adults. Her mouth grew dry and she wished she'd poured her own glass of water, too. "I grew up in a large home with more sisters than anyone would expect to have. Our mother, of sorts, took all of us in and stressed the benefits of an education. Not only did she expect us to excel in school but, as adults, we're expected to pass the joy of learning to children everywhere."

He nodded. "Interesting. So you were in a children's home of sorts?"

She swallowed before giving him a smile. "Yes. I was."

"In the area?"

"No, in New York City."

He wrote something down before looking at her.

"You're a long way from home. How did you find your way to our state?"

She smiled and glanced down at her hands to hide the panic. The truth was a disaster and lying was worse but she had no choice. "Well, you see, my brother wanted me to live with—"

The door burst open, the knob banging against the wall with the force. Henry stood there with his arms wide. "Honey, I'm home. Gimme a little sugar."

Mr. Bromley said, "This can't be your brother."

"What?" Henry scoffed. "Pffft, naw. I'm her husband. She's my wonderful little wife." He shuffled over to where she sat and bent to wrap his arms around her neck. "Best little wife in the world."

Sally gritted her teeth against the overwhelming whiskey fumes. She glanced over at Mr. Bromley as he stood and went for the door. "Sir, if you'll wait a moment, I can explain who this is."

"Sir?" Henry slurred. "I'm your darlin'," he said and kissed her cheek.

"Shut up and go lay down," she hissed. "I'll deal with you later." She shoved him from her and hopped to her feet. Mr. Bromley already had his hat in hand. "No, Henry, my brother here, has a head injury. He's been a near idiot since birth. I didn't want to confess this to you, in case you had a prejudice against the infirm."

"I see." After giving her a hard stare, he put on his hat and shook his head. "Do you think this is my first time learning a potential new hire is actually married?"

He did seem a lot older and more experienced so she had to say, "No?"

"Correct. It is not." He pulled thin gloves from a jacket pocket. "I don't know the state of your marriage to Mr. Wigg here, and I don't care."

"DuBoise," Henry offered and Sally shushed him. "What?" he asked her. "We're the DuBoises now."

Bromley looked from Henry to Sally. "Like I said, I don't care. Instead, what I will do is put the entire state educational system on notice for a Miss Wigg or Miss DuBoise." He pushed down on his hat and opened the door.

She followed him. "Please, Mr. Bromley. You have to wait and let me explain. He and I aren't married, not truly, and we will get our annulment in less than a week. Please reconsider our interview."

He stepped out and paused. A flicker of hope began in Sally but evaporated when he said, "No. You lied and we can't have impressionable young minds swayed by a dishonest person. Good day, madam."

Henry shook his head and sat where Mr. Bromley had been. "Hoo, he is one stuffy shirt, isn't he?" He sniffed at the half full coffee cup. "You just gave him water? 'S probably why."

Sally's vision grew gray around the edges and she couldn't breathe. Her fingernails dug into the palms of her hands. "I wish I'd never laid eyes on you."

"What, darlin'?"

His slack jaw and slurred speech grated on her last nerve. She wanted to slap him and hated herself for the urge to be violent. "You've spent the past week opining on how I'm too good for you. About how I deserve a better life than the one you can provide and, after today's little trick? You're right."

"I know I am."

She lifted her chin and glared down her nose at him. Henry sat there, sloppy, dumb, and happy. "You'll be in Sacramento by tomorrow and what sort of good will that do us? We'll have two rents and I can't find a job now because of you."

"Wha?" He frowned and tried to focus. "You have the interfew tomorrow."

Ignoring his mispronunciation, she shook her head. "The man you just ran off?" she asked and he nodded. "*He* was my interview." She sank into the chair opposite him. "He stopped by early to make sure I wasn't married."

"Oh."

After a few minutes of silence between them, she sighed. Her usually active mind was ground to a halt. She'd pinned everything on teaching in Oregon. If the superintendent had his way, she'd have to move to find employment or start her own school.

"I'm sorry."

"Don't be." She waved a hand, her eyes filling with tears. "I should have waited to marry you. Should have given myself more time to find out you're a drunk." He shuffled and sat up straighter. "No." She held up a hand for a second before wiping her cheeks. "Don't worry. I don't care how much you drink now. I'll go in tomorrow first thing and start the annulment proceedings."

"I'm not a drunk."

"Like I've said, what you are doesn't matter." She crossed her arms and stared out at the night sky from where they sat in the dark. At some point, she'd need to light the lamps. Right now, though, the effort seemed pointless. "You can go back to drinking every night once you're gone."

He laid his forehead down on the table. "I could. But, I don't drink and I don't want to leave."

Sally didn't want to argue about his drinking. "I

don't understand. You want to stay here, don't want to buy a farm or be married to me, and you come home drunk but don't drink."

"It's confusing," he muttered. "The boys found out about the promotion I don't know how. Someone blabbed and we had to go celebrate." He turned his head and rested his forehead on an arm. "Three whiskeys with ice and I'm finished, so I came home. You were here with that mister guy, so pretty and smiling at him."

She tilted her head. "You've been drunk twice, and the second time cost me my teaching dreams."

He moaned. "This is exactly why I don't drink. Pa couldn't handle his liquor and I can't handle mine." He looked up at her. "I'm sorry for what I did. The room isn't spinning and I'm not as happy now, but you're still the most beautiful woman I've ever seen. If you want me to buy you a school, it's yours."

She snorted and shook her head. He felt bad now, but tomorrow? He'd be back to wanting her gone. "What about your farm?"

"Doesn't matter. I believe in fixing my mistakes. I'll find you a school, buy it, and let you have your dream."

She stared into his eyes, her heart feeling squeezed inside her chest. He was willing to give her a school on a silver platter, yet, he couldn't return her love. She believed him about the drinking. No one who grew this intoxicated over a few drinks spent a lot of money on liquor.

The man wasn't a rascal who needed a wife to give him a reason to avoid the saloons. He needed a woman to be a partner. She wanted him to keep her as his but could already imagine what he'd say if she asked yet again. Her heart couldn't take another stern refusal. "No. Please don't. Teaching is not my only skill, I'll find other work. Meanwhile, it would be best for you to move to Sacramento."

CHAPTER NINE

Henry squeezed his already closed eyes harder. He didn't want to wake up to his second hangover in a year. *Hell*, he thought while pulling the covers over his head, the second hangover in a full decade. He'd left that life behind with his tall ship days.

His coworkers knew him as a teetotaler. He snorted, uncovering himself for more air. His abstinence was probably why they enjoyed buying him drinks so much. The intolerance for more than a couple of shots guaranteed them a good time. He'd all but danced the can-can last night.

And when he came home?

He groaned and put a hand over his face.

Sally. He'd ruined her chances for teaching in the *entire* state. To be fair, he hadn't known about the interview's date change. The festivities and cheering had left him in a good mood and he'd wanted to share the happiness with his new wife. He groaned again. The wife whose dreams he'd ruined.

Henry opened his eyes. Sally sat at the table, writing in her journal, and frowning. He winced. She was probably writing the foulest words about him. He cleared his throat, the sound echoing through his skull. "Good morning."

She glanced up at him for an instant before resuming her work.

So, she wasn't speaking to him. Henry couldn't blame her. "Would saying I'm extremely sorry help?"

She sighed before shaking her head.

"Damn," he muttered under his breath. She glared up at him before returning to giving him the silent treatment. If he weren't in serious pain, he'd want to sit and gaze at her all morning. She really was pretty, especially when angry. Her hair hadn't been wound into its usual handy bun. Instead, her locks flowed over her shoulders. Her gray blue eyes sparkled like St. Elmo's Fire. Plus, he could tell from the redness how she'd been biting her lip.

Henry went over and pulled out a chair across from her. The scrape echoed through every nerve in his body, stabbing each and every one of them. He winced and she glanced up with a slight smile. He fell into the chair, glad his pain had helped her mood. "We need to talk, and, if you don't want to say anything, that's fine. I just need to clear the air between us."

Sally put down her pencil and interlaced her fingers. With her hands on her book, she said, "I don't think we need anything beyond an annulment. You've stated your feelings on our marriage and your life goals time and again. There is no reason to rehash any of it."

"But, I feel like I need to explain last night and why it happened."

"Again, there's no reason to talk. What's done is

done and can't be helped." They stared at each other for a few seconds before she picked up her pencil. "Now if you'll excuse me, I have to create a backup plan since this one didn't work." She shrugged and turned to a fresh page. "Which is something I should have done before even meeting you. I know better than to jump into anything with both feet."

This was it. She was done with him. All of a sudden, Henry realized pushing her away was very different from watching her *walk* away. If his head didn't hurt so blasted much, he'd be able to figure a way to reel her back in. She'd looked at him with loving eyes before today. She had to look at him that way again.

Or what? his conscience asked. What would he do if she left him for good?

"There's coffee on the stove. Help yourself," she muttered, still writing in her book.

"Thank you," he said and stood. The infernal scraping happened again. "I'm getting a rug for under the table."

"Um hm. I've never had the pleasure of drinking too much. Or even drinking for that matter, but from what I've heard, you're probably miserable right now."

He rubbed his forehead. "I am. It's horrible."

"Good."

He tried not to smile at the spiteful little tone in her voice as he picked up the coffee pot. "If you were in this much pain, I'd feel bad for you."

"Oh, I feel horrible for you. Not only are you ill, you're losing a good partner." She stood and went over to take the coffee pot from his shaky hand. "I'm a hard worker, a great wife, an excellent instructor, and was over the moon for you." When his cup was full, she set down the pot. "After our annulment, I'll be free to find a husband who can appreciate me as much as I appreciate him."

Hearing his opinion but in Sally's words gutted him. He'd been indifferent at best, cruel at worst, to his hopeful bride. She'd had enough, it seemed, and he couldn't blame her. "You deserve a good man, I'll agree."

"All right." She took a step back. "I've been working on a plan this morning. Once you leave for Sacramento, I will have no reason to stay here, especially since I can't teach."

He took a sip of the somewhat cool coffee and frowned. "I don't mind paying for this apartment until you decide where to go."

"Thank you, but no. I'm an able-bodied woman and don't need your charity."

Henry stopped halfway in sitting down on the bed before continuing to the mattress. "It's not charity if you're my wife."

"Um hmm, I'm not your wife." She waved a dismissive gesture at him and went to the table. Picking up her journal and pencil, she continued, "At any rate, since you know I have my own money, I can use it to travel somewhere else. I can tell people I'm a widow and find employment in any other state but Oregon."

"You could come south with me," he offered. "Find a job like you'd planned and we'd share a home."

"As we are now, only in a different place?" she asked and when he nodded, she shook her head. "No. There's no need." She went and drained the last of the coffee into his cup. "We'll get an annulment and I'll go with being a widow. Accidents happen all the time. I'll dye my good dress black, get a teaching position, and move on from this debacle."

He glanced at her peach colored dress where it hung over a curtain rod she'd fashioned. She'd been wearing the dress when they'd met and he had never seen a woman so beautiful. He couldn't let Sally wear black and pretend to be one of the ladies he'd seen after the war; gray and lifeless without their husbands. "No."

"No what?"

"No to any of this." He drained his cup and stood. "I forbid you to do anything but stay married to me. I'll find a piece of land for both of us. I'll farm, you'll teach, and we'll be a true couple."

Sally stared at him for a few seconds before laughing. "Really? This is your decision?"

He went to her and put the cup on the table. "It is. I was wrong to deny how I feel for you. I want both of us to get what we want out of life, even if I have to hand saw trees to build a home and a school."

Expressions flickered across her face, like sunlight dancing on ocean waves. At last, she stood. "No, Henry. Now you merely want what you can't have. You don't think I can cope with farm life and maybe you're right. Maybe there's more to working outdoors than a bullheadedness to accomplish a task."

Was she right? Did he only want her now that he couldn't have her? He searched his heart and memory. No, he'd wanted her this entire time. "I...." His voice cracked, so he cleared his throat and said again, "I might have been wrong, Sally. You're perfect as you are. Too perfect, in fact, for me to believe you'd ever want to marry a sea dog turned farm hand like me."

He stepped up to her and placed his hand on her upper arm. "I'm sorry about the drinking. If you stay, I'll never touch another drop. I'll be the best husband in the world. I'll never let you have a cold day or hungry night."

She searched his face for a few seconds. "Are you saying such things to have me stay here while you work elsewhere? Keep up the place while you're gone?"

Henry slid his fingertips down her arm to hold her hand. She pulled away from his touch and turned away from him. He wanted her to face him, look into her eyes, and ask if he'd really lost her for good. Instead, he said, "No, not live here. I want you to live with me and be my wife."

Still not facing him, she asked, "If you don't hide me, won't people know we're married?"

"Everyone I work with knows about you." He ran a hand through his hair and sat on the edge of the bed. "Lucky and his family know. Mr. Granville knows about you. I'm really bad at keeping a secret, I suppose. Plus, I don't want to hide you from anyone. If anything, you should be hiding me."

He glanced up at her. She didn't move or say anything for a couple of minutes, and the tension coiled within him. Maybe she hadn't heard his near apology. "Sally?"

"I suppose I should wash up." She turned to him. "Do you want to wait until later to eat?"

He put a hand to his stomach. Nothing was making him nauseous, but he wasn't hungry, either. "Yes, please. Maybe dinner? I could take you to the

Harvey House."

She smiled and picked up the wash pail. "I'll cook. You need to save your money for moving and your future land." She grabbed his coffee mug, too. "Gather any clothes you want me to wash and I'll start on them this afternoon."

Henry nodded and she left the room, locking up afterward. He bent and put his head in his hands. Had they known each other in person only a week? Sally seemed so much more a part of him that the short time indicated. She didn't have his heart. She *was* his heart.

He sighed before lying down, and put his hands behind his head. A schoolhouse-farmhouse combination sounded perfect to him. He'd find the land somewhat near his sister's home; she and Sally would get along perfectly. He could ask Monsieur DuBoise, Del's father, for advice. With Sally being an orphan, she might want to adopt a few children. He didn't mind as long as they had one or two of their own. He closed his eyes and smiled. He hadn't dared of think about her in an intimate way, she seemed too above him. But, if she wanted a true marriage, who could blame him for desiring her in every way?

Her coffee had helped eased the pounding in his head. Now if she could only help the pounding in his heart.

***

Sally straightened and moved her head side to side. She'd have to find a better way of washing dishes than bent over a washtub. Especially now, when the days were turning cooler. Sooner than she'd like, they'd be busting through ice to get to the trough's water.

"My, my, isn't this a sight for my sore eyes?"

She jumped at the voice, her stomach turning over from him catching her here. "Good morning. I was just finishing up my washing."

He strolled up next to her, a little too close, and leaned over. "Looks like I missed watching you wash your delicates. Such a shame."

"I don't have any," she said and his eyes widened. Aghast at him thinking she wore nothing underneath, she quickly scrambled back. "I mean, I don't wash my delicates in public."

"That's too bad." He shifted to block her way back to the porch. "What's your hurry? Can't a man talk to a pretty girl once in a while? It's been a few days since we met. I've missed you."

Hairs on the back of her neck rose. She swallowed to remove the metallic taste in her mouth. "Sorry to hear that, but I really must be going."

"Why? You live alone." He reached out to wrap a stray curl from her temple around his finger. "No one to hurry to except me." He pulled her closer despite the tub she used as a shield. "I can talk all day."

His touch, harsh and repellant, sickened her. She looked around to see if anyone was nearby to ask for help. "I'm glad you have the free time but I don't. Please let me by."

"What will you do if I say no? Scream?"

She leaned away to avoid his stale breath. "Maybe."

"Go ahead. No one will hear you and, if they do, no one will care." He knocked the tub from her hands. Metal and porcelain crashed to the ground. "Now come here and give me some sugar."

Sally tried to block his face with her hand. "I said

no. Let me go!" She struggled and tried to resist him lowering her arm to her side. Now pinned down, she glared at him. "Let. Me. Go."

He laughed and leaned in for a kiss. A door slammed behind him and he paused to look up and say, "Move on. This doesn't concern you."

"It does when you're touching my wife."

Sally gasped, "Henry, please help me."

The brute looked from her to Henry and snorted. "Your wife? Little lady told me she didn't have a husband."

"Well, she does, and I want you to get your paws off of her." He pulled Sally from the man's grip.

She looked from her husband to her assailant. The large and threatening man seemed a lot less scary next to him. The two glared at each other while Henry rolled up his sleeves. She didn't want him to fight anyone, especially over a pretend wife. "Let's just go." She began picking up the spilled dishes and broken coffee cup. "It's not worth a fuss."

"I think some jackass handling my wife warrants a huge fuss." He sidestepped and pulled her behind him. His hands fisted in preparation as he faced the stranger. "Now, you can either leave or take your lumps."

"I should knock you halfway to China, but I won't. I'm a decent man and don't chase after married ladies." He straightened his jacket. "Next time, ma'am, speak up about your husband so no one gets the wrong idea."

Henry took a step forward, hands still ready to punch. "Next time, swine, when any lady says no, she means no."

With a last glare at both of them, the man turned

and left. Once he was out of earshot, Sally said, "Thank you for coming down. I didn't encourage him at all."

He turned to her with a frown. "Think so? Then why didn't you tell him you were married? He'd have left you alone."

Her mouth dropped open for a moment before she knelt and began picking up the broken dishes. "He talked to me soon after you'd told your family friend I was *Miss Wigg* and a short-term guest. I didn't know if you two had met. If I said we were married and you found out..." She looked up at him for a moment and then resumed picking up broken china. "I didn't want to make you any more irritated with me than you already were."

He squatted and helped clean up the mess. "I didn't know him and even if I did, any time you need to fib to keep yourself safe, do it. Lie like a rug if you have to keep a snake like him away from you." He looked over at her. "Understand? I'll agree to anything if it means your safety."

She smiled and nodded. His concern helped thaw her earlier anger over his actions yesterday. He picked up the last bit of broken ceramic from the coffee cup and she put her hand on his. "Thank you. I'll try to be as honest as I can. I'd hate for you to have to go along with a lie you didn't start."

He pulled his hand from hers to help her stand. "I don't care. Whatever you need to do is fine with me." He drew her into a brief hug. "Now, let's get an inventory and list what needs replacing. We might want to add another coffee cup for you."

"We've been making do with a single set of dishes."

"You have, and it shows what a bum I've been in caring for you." He followed her up the stairs, the glass shards clinking against the metal pan. "Anyone else would have thought about supplying his wife with everything she needed before she arrived."

"You could have, but let's think of it as you gave me a choice instead of choosing my dishes for me." She tried to unlock the door to find he hadn't locked it before coming down. "We could also use two keys so I can go shopping while you're at work."

He chuckled and set the tub on the table. "That sounds like a good idea until I think about what my store credit would be each time."

She bit her lip as her face grew warm. "You might have a point." She watched as he went to lock the door. "I rarely ever shop for myself, and buying things for you sounds fun."

Henry took a few steps toward Sally before taking her in his arms. He held her close and whispered in her ear, "Do you know what else sounds fun? Kissing my wife." He brushed his lips over hers in the lightest of touches. "Does she want to kiss her husband?"

Sally shivered as his breath tickled her ear. Memories of their first kiss crowded her mind and left her breathless. She pressed her cheek against his, sliding back until their lips almost met. "She does."

CHAPTER TEN

The next morning, Sally stirred, turning over while under the heavy blankets. She'd had the best dream, only.... She opened her eyes to find Henry, also in bed, staring at her with a smile. They'd become a true husband and wife last night. The annulment would be impossible unless they lied.

"Good morning, sunshine."

His sleepy and satisfied voice made her whole body come alive. "Good morning. I suppose we should talk."

He smoothed her unbound hair from her face. "I don't know. Seems like doing is much more fun than talking."

Her face burned at the suggestion in his tone and she covered her head with the blankets. He laughed and she couldn't help but smile at his amusement. She peeked out of the cocoon. "We really shouldn't have."

"Probably not." He reached out under their blankets and drew her into his arms. "It's a mistake I'd gladly make again this morning."

The idea of repeating last night left her a little breathless. His warm body lured her closer so she snuggled up to him. She breathed in his clean scent and murmured against his skin, "Do you have to work today?"

He kissed the top of her head. "No. I had planned on packing and getting ready to leave on the last train tonight."

"Had?" She paused in running her fingers through his chest hair. "Are you turning down the job to stay here?"

"Not exactly." He caressed her back. "I'd like for you to pack, too, and move with me. Be my wife in Sacramento."

She stilled. Considering how much he'd protested their marriage after meeting her, his change in heart puzzled her. Not that she minded his reversal but did he want her to move back to Oregon when he found a farm up here? Or had he planned on leaving her in Sacramento and alone? She needed to know for sure. "I'm not sure I *want* to be married to you."

He chuckled and combed her hair with his fingers. "It's too late. We already are and in every way."

Snuggled against him, Sally had to agree being a wife was better than she'd expected. Yet, she had a life goal beyond being Mrs. Henry DuBoise. "If we stay together, I can't teach until we build my school."

"You're my wife. There's no need for you to teach."

She couldn't help but snort at his arrogance and threw it right back at him. "You're my husband. There's no need for you to farm."

He turned over to lie on his back, letting her go, and she already missed his touch. He closed his eyes.

"Very well. I don't want to leave you here, not now. But, the offer is too good to pass up. I can make enough to finance both of our goals."

His including her dreams with his warmed her to her toes. She nestled in against his shoulder. "I can stay here and look for farmland. Or, you could look where you are and maybe find a place."

"Would you move to be with me?"

She turned her head to look at him. He hadn't opened his eyes. Would she? The offer tempted her. Goodness knows the sisters she was closest to lived south of her. They'd be able to see each other far more often, especially Rebecca, way down in Texas. She missed her the most.

But, he'd been so adamant about not marrying her, though, and the denials still stung. "Would you want me to stay married to you?"

The silence stretched for a minute before he said, "I do, but I can't want to keep you. You deserve better."

He was back to that frail excuse again. She rolled her eyes, disgusted with his dodges and with her foolish hopes. "Fine. We'll stay married. I'll find a job in a laundry or cannery while you work in Sacramento." She climbed over him, the struggle to ignore his body nearly overwhelming. "You buy your farm. I start my school. Then, we divorce. Simple as that."

"Sounds like the best plan to me."

She frowned at him while she pulled her dress on. Her shaky fingers fumbled with the buttons. "I'm glad you approve."

"Good."

Tears filled her eyes and her nose stung. She stood

and went to start coffee for them. Last night had been magical for her and obviously nothing much for him. The coffee beans clattered in the pot, jangling her nerves. The cold stove echoed the emotional chill in the room. By this time tomorrow, she'd be waking up to an empty bed.

***

Henry kept his eyes closed through Sally's stoking the fire and heating coffee. Last night with her had been the stuff of dreams. No man deserved such heaven. He'd found his life mate and was convinced he couldn't be hers. Although... He rolled over onto his side and pushed the thought away. No. No excuses or rationalizing. She deserved her school and a better husband.

His conscience tried to argue and he opened his eyes to shut it up. She wore her work dress. The drab brown didn't enhance but also couldn't detract from her beauty. He sighed and threw off the covers to begin dressing. She'd have breakfast started, they'd eat, and he'd go get everything ready to leave on the last train south tonight.

"I'll make extra at dinner. Meals on the train and at the stations are expensive."

He stood and pulled on his pants. "Thank you. It'll get us to our goals that much faster." He walked over to her while slipping on his shirt. "You don't have to work in a laundry or in the cannery. Especially not the cannery. I can provide for the both of us."

Sally put a cup of coffee on the table for him before turning back to the frying pan and eggs. "No, I want to. A little hard work never hurt anyone." She smiled at him. "Not even me."

He liked her teasing far more than her hurt or

anger. Still, he was the man of their little family. The word stopped his fingers from the last button. Family? What if.... He turned away, his legs a lot weaker now, and sank into the kitchen table's chair. He might have to come back in a few months.

A lump formed in his throat and he coughed before saying, "I might need to move here sooner than I'd planned, if..." She turned to him with a questioning frown. He tried to smile. "You know, in case last night was something more than we had expected. You know, *expected*."

Her eyebrows rose as fast as her jaw dropped. Her mouth formed a thin line before she said, "You might, but I hope not. That sort of surprise will ruin everything."

She went back to her cooking while he sat there, his mind full of the children possible between them. All of the girls would be beautiful like her. He hoped the boys turned out to be as stubborn as Sally, too. They'd go far in life with her determination. He scooted the chair closer to the table. "Maybe I should stay here for a month or two before leaving."

"I don't think there's a need and I don't think they'll hold the job for you that long."

"What if we, um, last night, and you might..." he tried to say.

She began putting food on two folded dishtowels for them. "From what I've seen, even if the worst happened, you'd have a good four months at work paying you nearly double." She shrugged and sat down with her food. "We shouldn't have to change our plans due to one mistake."

He cut the egg into smaller and smaller pieces. A child of theirs might be unexpected but could never be a mistake. He nibbled at a bite, suddenly not hungry. Why did *his words* coming *from her* always hurt him? He'd say they needed to separate and he didn't ache. She'd tell him she wanted out of their marriage and his heart seemed to tear out of his chest.

Henry stabbed into a bit of egg white before eating it. She wasn't picking at her food like he was. She'd glance at him with a smile every so often and he tried to grin in response. Finishing first, she took her towel to the washtub and asked, "Would you like the rest of the coffee?"

"Yes, if you've had enough."

She came over and filled his cup. "I have, thank you." She paused for a couple of seconds while looking at him. "I suppose if the worst happened, I could always come to you. That way, we'd only be paying rent on one home."

He wanted to protest her point of view about their possible child, but, she was right about the situation not being ideal. "I'd like that. You might could come with me anyway."

Sally shook her head and opened yesterday's newspaper. "No, or more nights together might happen and we can't take the chance."

"I liked last night a lot and that's sort of my point."

Her face reddened. "As did I, but more of that and we might as well get used to never being apart." She folded the paper to show just the classifieds. "The children will force us into a marriage you don't want."

"I…" he began to protest before stopping. She was right. And yet, very wrong. He drank the last of his coffee. "I'll be back as often as I can to visit. Just so men remember you're married and to leave you alone."

She glanced up from the paper before resuming her reading. "You don't have to, but discouraging the others would be nice."

Henry nodded. He owed Sally her safety. Watching the expressions on her face while she read the paper, he had to urge to call off everything and stay with her. A part of him wanted to accept her claim of being a good farmer's wife or even give up his dream of farming. He'd never hated fishing salmon, really. He'd just wanted a patch of solid land near a river. That way, he'd be able to sail a smaller boat while raising crops and children with Sally.

He reacted with a start as if he'd fallen asleep in church. No, she wasn't going to be the mother of his children. When this month proved unfruitful, and it had to, he'd allow her to move on and find a husband worthy of her. In fact, he needed to encourage her to find someone else while he was gone.

His entire body hurt at the thought of losing her to anyone else, but it was for her own good. He sat up to get ready to tell her about his idea when he caught the expression on her face. She stared at the paper, shaking her head, and he asked, "What's wrong?"

"You can't leave Portland because I've found your farm," Sally said, transfixed on the newspaper.

"What?"

"They're asking a little less than your savings. It has a house, a barn, and is somewhat close to Oregon City."

CHAPTER ELEVEN

Henry listened as she continued about the location, the cost, the home, and barn. The owner had died with no relatives and the land was up for sale.

"Do you know?"

He glanced up from the cold eggs. "I'm sorry?"

"Do you know who lived there?"

"Let's see the description," he replied and she handed the paper to him. He read the legal description and directions. "Sounds like the Nelson farm, but it's been a while. If I went out there, I'd probably know for certain." He saw the price. The cost, nearly four thousand dollars, equaled what they had together. "Did you see what price they're asking for?"

"I did." She leaned forward, her hands on the table. "We should go see the home and land before you pack. What if it's your dream come true but you miss it by leaving today?"

"I don't know."

"Even worse, you go visit your family, ride past and find out it was your perfect farm but you lost your chance at a dream?" She stared into his eyes. "You don't want to miss the best thing to ever happen to you, do you?"

"No, I don't suppose not," he answered and her face relaxed into a smile. "We could go just to see if I know the seller."

"Wonderful. I'll change into my best dress." Sally stood and hurried to her carpetbag. "We can go and be back before you leave." She turned to him. "If you'll still want to, that is."

She had such a hopeful expression on her face. It echoed the feeling in his chest, the impending absence. "Maybe. I'm not getting my hopes up."

"I understand. You've probably been disappointed before." She shook out her dress with a smile. "Not every surprise is a bad one. Sometimes, when you're expecting great things, you'll find you can be happy with merely good."

He watched as she smoothed out the wrinkles in her skirt before kicking off her shoes. He'd have been a lot happier with a *good* woman. Instead, he married an amazing one. Leaning back in his chair, he asked, "Will you change clothes in front of me?"

Her face turned a deep red as she tucked down her chin. "Sorry, I was focused on making our dreams come true and forgot my modesty."

"It's all fine from where I'm sitting, ma'am." He couldn't help but chuckle at her gasp. "But if it'll help your delicate sensibilities, I'll turn around when I change, too."

"Thank you."

Henry chuckled as he went to retrieve his best shirt and pants. Making good on his promise to give her some privacy, he went to the other side of the room. He undressed down to his underpants before glancing back at her. She stared at his undress as much as he drank in her in a thin chemise.

She let out a squeak when their eyes met before she turned around, too.

He couldn't help but let out a low whistle at his attractive wife. "I almost don't care about going anywhere but back to bed with you."

"Oh, well, I guess neither of us got enough sleep last night. We should go see your farm anyway, don't you think?"

Chuckling at hearing the embarrassment in her voice, he couldn't help but continue teasing her. "Sure, I'll put on my boots since you'd rather ride around the country instead of ride around in bed with me."

"Henry!"

She was fully dressed by the time he turned around. All of his goals, once set in stone, now seemed made of quicksand. His heart wasn't in Sacramento, it was right here, standing in front of him in a peach dress. "We'll need to rent a buggy. At some point, I'll need to buy a wagon and horses, when I buy the farm." She giggled and he grinned at the sound. "I mean, purchase the farm, not die, or anything."

"I'm sure." She put on her hat and grabbed her carpetbag. "How far is the livery stable from here?"

"Not too far. A half mile or so." He led her into the hall and locked up.

"Do you walk to work and back every day?"

He nodded and held the main door open for her. "I'll hitch a ride when the weather's bad." She smiled and took his arm as they walked. Her body brushed his every so often and dissolved any concentration he might have had.

Their love last night wouldn't leave his mind. His skin still tingled everywhere she'd touched him. He glanced at her. The woman kept getting prettier day by day. He put an arm around her to protect against a group of men. He almost resented having to share her company with anyone today. When was sunset, again?

"Did we pass the stable?" She turned and looked behind them. "I think so."

"Sure did. I was thinking too hard." He grinned at her chuckle and led her inside the large building. "Hey, Garner. I need to hire a horse and cart for the day."

"Sure thing." He glanced from Henry to Sally while grabbing a receipt pad and pencil. "Just a cart or would you rather have a nice buggy for the lady here?"

He'd known Roger Garner since his family arrived in Oregon. Earlier, he could deny his marriage, but after last night? He didn't want to. Besides, she deserved respect as a married lady instead of scorn for riding alone into the countryside with a man. He gave Roger a grin. "Aw, you know buggies are for courting a girl. Carts are for when she's already married you."

"Well, this gal's your wife?" He turned to Sally. "I'd congratulate you, ma'am, but it's this varmint who needs the congratulations. He married way above his station."

"Thank you, but no. I'm lucky to have him, too." She smiled at Roger, gave Henry a glance before turning away to look out of the window.

He swallowed a lump in his throat. She didn't seem happy to him, and he hoped telling Roger she was his wife was all right. "Yeah, I have her fooled. And since we're newlyweds, maybe I'd better get that buggy after all."

"Good deal. I have just the one in mind." The man began scribbling. "Give the top copy to Jed out back and keep the bottom for yourself. Deposit is fifty dollars but I'll give you a honeymoon special and just charge the five for rental."

"Thank you." He took the receipt. "If I'd known I'd get discounts from you, I'd have married years ago." He took the receipt. "We should be back before dinner."

"I'm not worried. Have a good time, and nice to meet you, ma'am."

"Nice to meet you, too." Sally followed Henry out to the main barn. "Sometime, I want to ask why you haven't married before now."

"Sure." His throat suddenly dry, he swallowed. She might as well know why he was so dead set against their marriage. The reason was tough to think, never mind admit to anyone else. He walked up to a young man not much older than his younger brother. "Hey, Jed."

"Henry. Let's see what you got." He took the receipt as if entitled to it. "He's put you in the nice cart today. Plus Tanner is our finest horse." He glanced up and gave back the paper. "Meet me out front."

He nodded and smiled at Sally. "Shall we?" She nodded and he went to the front of the building with her. "Jed's a good man. We worked together on the fishing boats before he went lame."

"I noticed he had a slight limp. I hope he's improving with time," she said as the buggy turned the corner.

Henry grinned. Roger had given him the finest vehicle at a wagon price. Jed hopped down and gave Henry the reins. "Thank you." After a tip of the hat, he moseyed on over to Sally. "Let me help you up?"

"Yes, please."

She gave him a gloved hand and gathered her skirt. Soon, he was seated next to her and clicking at the horse to go. They headed out south of town as he asked, "Did you bring the paper with you?"

"I did." She rummaged around in her bag and pulled out the page. "It says the place is five miles or so northeast of Oregon City, Nelson farm."

"I know exactly where it is. We came to Oregon with the Nelsons, and I'm sorry to hear they're gone. No one ever said if their son Jimmy made it back here after the war." He glanced over as she put the paper back in her bag. Fabric from her work dress caught his eye, as did her journal.

So. She continued to keep all of her belongings in her carpetbag. He sighed and stared ahead. If he'd been home from dawn to dusk, he'd have probably noticed before now, except, no, he hadn't. He subconsciously shook his head before realizing what he was doing. She'd been afraid to unpack due to his constant denials of keeping her as his wife.

The hour passed with him wanting to talk with her but being afraid to broach any subject. He'd glance over at her, but Sally seemed more interested in the passing scenery than in him. Not until they pulled up in front of the old Nelson place did he offer, "My sister and her family lives nearby."

"Is that good?"

He hopped down from the buggy and reached for her. "Yes and no. How much would you like your in-laws?"

She smiled while letting him help her to the ground. "Depends on how much I'd like my husband, I suppose."

Henry did not want to fall in that pit of conversation. He wanted to stay her husband but couldn't, wanted her to love him like she shouldn't, and wanted to say he loved her yet wouldn't. He glanced over at her as she looked around the farm.

She seemed impressed and he smiled, saying, "The Nelsons had invited us over when I was younger. It's been fifteen years or so. I've forgotten about the inside of the buildings." They walked toward the house, first, and he continued, "The outside has changed some. There are new trees in some places and several old trees are gone."

"Do you remember if they made a good living here?" she asked while walking up on the porch. She peeked in the windows while knocking on the door. "I hope they have someone watching the place until it's sold."

"So do I." He peeked in, too, while they waited. "I wonder if Jimmy is even in the country. He was the only one close to my age. The rest of them were older." After a minute more, he walked over to the window. Dust covered everything the sheets didn't.

Sally walked up next to him. "They've been gone a while."

"I'm not surprised. None of us were close after the war, and I never saw any of them after I enlisted."

"I forget you're old enough to have fought."

He grinned at her. "Barely and I had to lie. But yeah." He motioned toward the other building. "Let's see if the barn is open."

They walked on together. She said, "I wouldn't know what to look for in a wood house's quality."

"I'd like to see more before we buy anything." The barn door swung open, thanks to the broken latch. "Looks like there's a lot to do before planting season." He went in first. Sunlight streamed in through the opposite end where the door seemed missing altogether. "Lots to do for sure."

"Come on, don't tell me you're already afraid of hard work." She walked on into the building. "Mr. I-love-hard-labor and all?" She turned to give him a teasing look. "I'd expect you to be sad everything's not a heap of rubble."

He laughed. "I might have overstated my love of working hard."

"A little, yes." She turned back to looking at everything. "Still, the roof seems solid and there's not huge cracks in the wood. That has to be something in the farm's favor."

"If the well isn't dry, and I'll bet it isn't, the place is a good deal for the price." He followed as she led him out into the midday sun.

"I think north of the barn would be a perfect place for a school. Just classrooms for the first floor and as it grows, we can add a second story for bedrooms for children needing homes as well as an education."

Children needing homes? Ice water flowed in his veins. He'd forgotten how she might already be carrying their baby. All of a sudden, he couldn't breathe. They'd buy land together, she'd have his children, they'd take in more stray children and what then? He'd be like his father. "No."

"No?" She went to stand in front of him. "No to what, Henry? You're pale and I know it's not hot enough to sweat as much as you are. What's wrong?"

He couldn't be honest with her. Honesty meant saying the darkest parts of him out loud to her. It was one thing to say he wasn't good enough for Sally, another to say the words why. "All this work for a woman like you isn't right. We can go on back because I have a train to catch."

Her jaw hung open for a second. "No, I'd like to stay here and figure out why you're so rattled. Did something bad happen here and you won't tell me?"

"Nothing happened." He tried to make his shrug casual. "Nothing at all."

She frowned at him. "All right, I'll try to believe you, but your hard work excuses are wearing thin. You do realize that washing huge loads of laundry in a vat or canning salmon is as difficult as plowing a field must be."

He shook his head, unable to agree with her. "Does women work in a city leave blisters as much as farm work does?" He crossed his arms. "I don't think so."

Sally stared at him for a couple of seconds before pulling off her gloves. "I'm surprised you didn't notice before last night, but I truly am not afraid of hard work." She showed him her bared palms. "I didn't want to come to you with nothing and Madam Wiggie couldn't afford a lot of money with each of us girls."

Henry'd had and seen worse callouses before now, but never imagined Sally had them, too. His heart broke for how hard she must have worked for her hands to be so rough. He reached out and traced a finger over her thickened skin. "You're right. I should have noticed before now." He looked up and went on to caress her face with the back of his hand. "My only excuse is you keep me distracted with your beautiful eyes." He grinned and brushed a thumb over her mouth. "The kisses, too, leave me goofy for hours afterward." He pulled her into a hug. "I'm sorry I didn't look closer at you, all of you."

"Don't fret too much," she said against his shoulder. "I didn't make an effort to show you my ugly side."

Henry chuckled. "Darlin', I've seen most of you and you have no ugly side." He squeezed her tighter. "And I'm impressed with the land here, but no. The house needs a lot of work and I'd like to work in Sacramento for a little more money." He heard and felt her gasp but couldn't give her a chance to object. "I want you to join me there instead of staying here. You can work there, or not, as long as you're with me."

She pulled back to stare at him. "So you do love the farm?"

"Yes, I do. This just isn't the right time."

"We have the money. This is the place, and we are married so everything seems pretty clear to me." She left his arms to take a few steps backward. "You're the one who's afraid of hard work. You've used every excuse and left out the real reason you won't stay with me and buy this place."

Her anger spread to him, her words pecking at his ego like a colony of angry seagulls. Henry had traveled the Oregon Trail as a boy and lost his mother when his sister was kidnapped. He'd been in the end of the Civil War and watched his friends die. The idea he was afraid of anything cut deep. "All right. What's my reason?"

"You're chicken."

CHAPTER TWELVE

The longer Henry glared at Sally, the more she wanted to take the words back. How many times had she been scolded for giving in to anger? Still, she couldn't apologize because she wasn't sorry. He knew this was a good place for an excellent price. The house was sturdy, the barn was rather solid, and they had the money to live the rest of the year here. The place was their dreams come true. And yet he said no.

"I am not chicken." He crossed his arms and stared over her head. "I merely love you too much to let you be a farmer's wife."

Sally chuckled until realizing he'd said he loved her. He'd shown his feelings all along, yet, her heart melted when he said the words out loud. She didn't know why, but he truly was scared and not just about committing to her or the land. He gave her a sharp glare and she shook her head. "I didn't mean to laugh. You seem to not know all of my past."

"I know enough. You're very educated, refined,

and too good to be trapped out here in the middle of a corn field. I can't let you be an ordinary farmer's wife no matter how much you seem to want to."

The idea of growing corn alarmed her a little. She'd never read a book on how to do so. Shrugging off the anxiety, she focused on Henry. She had to get him out of his defensive stance. "I'm also an ordinary orphan who grew up in a school of other abandoned children. My sisters and I only had each other and Madam Wiggie."

"You have sisters? How many? Do they all live in New York City?"

"Yes, there are twenty-four of us, starting schools all over the country. One lives in Marshville just south of here, another in California, and one in Texas." She put her hands on his upper arms and looked deep into his eyes. Their crisp blue held her captive every time, and she smiled. "You might want to be an ordinary farmer and I might be an ordinary teacher, but together we're extraordinary." She lifted up to give him a brief kiss. "Don't you think so?"

"I do." He drew her closer. "Are you sure you can let your school be here instead of anywhere else?"

"If this is your new farm, it's my new home, too." She snuggled in against him. "Would it be possible for you to keep me as your wife?"

"Maybe."

His indecision hurt and her eyes filled with tears. "All right. I'll take what I can."

He groaned and hugged her tighter. "Sally, you don't know what you're in for with me."

"Aren't you a good man, apart from the drinking?"

"It's not that at all." He let go of her to hold her at arm's length. "I need to tell you something so you'll know all of this is no good."

A tremor of fear ran through her. Something had to be so bad for him to deny what they felt for each other. "All right. Tell me and let me have a choice in my fate, too."

"My father drank a lot. He'd finish off the medicine whiskey and hunt down more. Sometimes he was happy after emptying a pint, most times he wasn't. The only time I have a drop is around others. Even then, it's one or two. Three if I'm pressured. It's why I can't hold my liquor."

"You don't drink enough to be able to, do you?" she said more than asked. Thinking back on his hangovers, something else became clearer to her. "You're afraid of becoming your father when you start a family."

He nodded and turned away from her. "I am. Everyone said he was a good man until he married my mother. His first wife died when Ellen was a child, and Pa remarried. My sister never talked much about it, but I remember the bad times."

"You must have had hope. Otherwise, you'd have never advertised in the Bulletin for a bride."

Henry chuckled and faced her again. "I was on a mission. A plain ole farm gal out here would keep me busy with chores and raising children far too much to live in a saloon. When you stepped off the train, it was like I'd met a woman far better than I ever deserved." He shook his head. "You'd need to live in town, near saloons, to teach school."

Sally felt sure he believed what he was saying, but she wasn't certain of her own faith. And, she didn't want to consider him marrying anyone else. "I'd prefer you not mentioning any other woman keeping you busy from now on. Instead, I am going to insist that, since you love me and I love you, we buy the land and live our lives."

"You're not worried about my drinking?"

She stepped up to him. "I won't lie, I will worry."

"I don't crave drinking like Pa did, and yet…"

"It's a concern." She put her arms around him. "Your idea of keeping a woman busy out here does sound like a wonderful solution." Her cheeks grew hot, but she ignored the shyness and said, "I'd like to stay as occupied as we were last night."

"So would I." He leaned in and kissed her.

When their lips met, she held him and let the kiss deepen. A train whistle sounded in the distance. She broke the kiss and murmured, "We need to decide soon."

"Would you want to meet my family? Your new family?"

She nodded, not trusting her voice as tears filled her eyes.

He pulled her into his arms again. "Let's go tell them there's a new DuBoise to welcome."

"And the farm?"

"I want to talk to my brother-in-law, make sure there are no surprises before we buy."

She smiled and took his hand. "Unless they're good ones?"

"Yes, good ones like you."

EPILOGUE

Dear Tillie,

I hope all is well with you and your beloved doctor. Henry and I are looking forward to meeting up with you both soon. Only, we have some happy news! We're to have our own little student in a few months! We're both thrilled to pieces.

The funny thing about Henry, and I can't wait to tell Uma and Rebecca when we meet, is how protective he is now. He went from insisting I toughen up with farm chores to insisting on bed rest. I'll confess I enjoyed lounging around for exactly two days. After that, I sent him to his sister's home for a good talking to from her. Even then, it took him another two days to admit I would be safe venturing outside. If he weren't so worried and besotted with me, I'd tell him where he could hang his restrictions.

I received a letter from Uma yesterday. She's fine but her need for vengeance and answers never ceases to worry me. I know our dear Wiggie gave her the best tools to cope with any danger, yet, I'd feel better if she weren't so far away from you and me.

And speaking of long distances, it's been a while since I've heard from Rebecca. So often, I wish she had found a groom closer to us. I suppose that's selfish, considering how happy she is.

All my best to you and do write soon!
Love,
Sally

BONUS MATERIAL
Rider's Desire

The first in a fresh new series! Follow Clay in Rider's Desire as he delivers mail for the Pony Express. A quick sneak peek!

Chapter One

Clay Winslow nodded at the stack of dusty letters in their postal box. "He never picked them up? Looks like a man lucky enough to have family might be a little more interested in what they write to him."

Daggart Bartlett shrugged. "It's not his family so much as a woman. I don't understand it, either, but maybe he's been married before and is a smarter man now."

"I heard that," said a woman from the back and behind the wall of post office boxes. "You'll be talking out of the other side of your mouth when you're hungry tonight."

He winked at Clay and said, "She loves me."

Mrs. Bartlett walked up to the cash register with one of her hands resting on a very pregnant belly. Clay figured she'd be a lot prettier if she were a lot less stern faced. "Ma'am," he said with a nod.

"Hello. Is he taking care of you or just jawing around as usual?" She didn't give him a chance to respond. "That man loves to talk a stone post to death."

"He's fine, Mary. No need to fuss."

"He's also a pony boy and is most likely needing you to hurry up so he can leave."

Clay couldn't hide his smile. "I'm good, ma'am.

The next bundle goes out first thing tomorrow morning."

"Hmph. Well, don't complain if you're still here by then."

The shopkeeper leaned in to Clay and said, "It's her condition making her extra crab—, uh, conscientious. That's all."

She shook her head and wandered out of the room. "Don't mind me. What do I know?"

Daggart pursed his lips and stared down at the counter until her footsteps faded. Giving Clay a grin, he said, "I tried my best to not love the woman. Have to admit, she smiles and I'm lying in the mud, waiting for her to find me again."

He figured there had to be a story behind Mr. Bartlett's mud comment but the letters bothered him. Clay had been a Pony Express rider for too long and their neglect wouldn't leave him alone. "Who's supposed to be picking up the mail no one wants?"

"These?" He reached back and grabbed the stack. "Richard Crandall had been pretty regular about reading and sending replies to this little ole gal from back east. I don't know what happened."

Clay frowned. He'd heard that name before now and tried to remember where. Daggart pulled the first and last letter. He pushed them both where Clay could read.

"They're arranged like they arrived. Rich told me a little bit about the lady he'd been writing. He seemed to like her enough to write once a month." Daggart looked behind him for a second before tapping the last letter sent. "Don't know if I like anyone that much."

He chuckled and tried to keep quiet so Daggart

didn't get grief from Mary again. "I'd have to be in a lot of love, too."

"Yeah, well." He stacked the letters, tapping them on the counter. "Avoid that mess as long as you can, Winslow. Else you'll end up in a general store and henpecked by a good woman."

"I'll keep that in mind." He nodded at the stack of goods. "How much do I owe you?"

"A dollar fifty."

Clay paid him, putting what he could in his pockets. "Thank you."

"You're welcome. Don't be a stranger, now."

He nodded and stepped aside as a couple walked into the store. Clay went outside, the sun bright in the late afternoon. Various buggies and wagons rolled up and down the street. The wheels kicked up dust and people hollered above the noise to be heard. He pushed his hat down, ready to be out in the wide open territories.

Tomorrow was his turn to ride from here to at least Yank's station. A little over a hundred miles, give or take a few. He'd need some rest before his turn tomorrow morning at four. Not everyone went for the daybreak run like him. They didn't know the beauty they missed like Clay did.

He walked down the boards. Creaks and footsteps of others moving around him created a music of sorts. The noise drowned out most of the other sounds until he stood in front of the saloon. A familiar tune bled through the closed doors and he grinned. A drink or two couldn't hurt. Hungover on a pony for most of tomorrow didn't appeal to him, no, but a nice warming sip sounded good right now.

Clay went in. The bar was empty with a couple of

die-hard regulars sitting on the end. One grinned and raised his glass in greeting. He nodded and settled for the middle of the bar. Later on, he would come in for a game or two of cards, serious drinking, and conversation. Right now, he wanted no demands or plans on his time.

The barkeep stepped up to him while wiping the counter with a rag. "What's the good word today, son?"

He grinned at the man old enough to be his grandfather. "Scotch. A finger or two of your best, Grady."

"That's all, or should I leave out the bottle for ya?"

"That's all." Clay put his elbows on the bar as Grady placed a mostly clean glass in front of him and poured. He slid a quarter to him and asked, "Have you seen Rich Crandall around here lately?"

"No, and none of us will." Grady scooped up the money. "Crandall was killed in that mine collapse last week. You might have been out of town then."

He nodded. Clay had been on the way back from the station at Cold Springs. "He's got a pile of letters at Bartlett's waiting for him."

"I'm not surprised. He had a little ole gal from back east sweet on him."

"Did he like her, too?"

"Suppose so. He'd come in, read to himself, scribble something down, and go back to the post office." Grady smeared dust around the countertop with a brown rag. "I never minded. He'd always have a glass or two. Sometimes three while writing her."

"I wonder if she knows what happened to him."

ABOUT THE AUTHOR

With an overactive imagination and a love for writing, Laura Stapleton decided to type out her daydreams and what if's. She currently lives in Kansas City with her husband and a few cats. When not at the computer, you'll find her in the park for a jog or at the yarn store's clearance section.

If you enjoyed this story, please consider leaving me a review. I'd love to learn more about my readers so if you prefer, you can contact me via the links below. I always welcome constructive advice and hoped you liked reading this story.

Find me online at
https://twitter.com/LauraLStapleton,
www.facebook.com/LLStapleton and at
http://lauralstapleton.com. Subscribe to my newsletter to keep up on the latest and join my Facebook group at Laura's Favorite Readers.

Manufactured by Amazon.ca
Bolton, ON